LAKEVIEW MOTEL

tales of the underinformed

Darryl Halbrooks

Copyright © 2004 by Darryl Halbrooks

Published by: UNIPRESS
Westcliffe CO 81252
and Instantpublisher.com

To order this or other works please visit:
www.darrylhalbrooks.com
or email dhalbro@aol.com

Printed in the United States of America 2004

ISBN 1-59196-812-7

All rights reserved. No part of this book shall be reproduced or transmitted in any form or by any means, electronic, mechanical, magnetic, photographic including photocopying, recording or by any information storage and retrieval system, without prior written permission of the publisher. No patent liability is assumed with respect to the use of the information contained herein. Although every precaution has been taken in the preparation of this book, the publisher and author assume no responsibility for errors or omissions. Neither is any liability assumed for damages resulting from the use of the information contained herein.

This is a work of fiction. Names, characters, places, and incidents either are the product of the author's imagination or are used fictitiously. Any resemblance to actual events or locales or persons, living or dead, is entirely coincidental.

for Carly and Mike

Contents

Battlefield Subdivision and Golf Community	1
Lakeview	9
Summit Fever	17
Scumbag	27
Gretchen of Wisconsin	39
Low-Rider	58
Spiderhole	70
Jim Joyce	87
The High Ground	103
Land of Many Uses	120
Arrowhead	137
Europa	145
C. and P. Charming	165
Singrid Advaard	174
Mr. Friendly	189

Acknowledgements

This book has benefited from the input of many friends as well as my editor whose time and good graces I have once again imposed upon for valuable criticism.

Note: *Gretchen of Wisconsin* first appeared in Slowtrains Literary Journal, Summer issue 2004

Darryl Halbrooks

Notes

Lakeview Motel

The characters in this collection are as flawed as in my previous two books. We can identify with and even sympathize with some of them them but others are such losers that we can only thank our lucky stars that circumstances allowed us to make better decisions and take different paths.

Illustrations: Cover design and illustrations: by the author.

Illustrations

Evening at Lakeview	cover
Jarred and Jennel	1
Evening at Lakeview2	9
Summit Ridge	17
Escape from Bar Tab	27
Snow Angel	39
Low Ride	58
Spiderhole	70
Crunchtime	87
Professor Hitler	103
Camp Randall	120
Nice Shot	137
Another Motel	145
C Charming	165
Hangar	179
Waiting Area	189

Lakeview Motel

Battlefield

Battlefield Subdivision and Golf Community

At 12:24 AM Tuesday, August 21, 1982, in the maternity ward of St. Elias Hospital, Jeremy Manson, a white male, weighing in at seven pounds-six ounces, made his way into this world. St Elias had also presided over the births of his parents, Hugh and Marilyn. Both parents were identical in pigmentation to little Jeremy. His great-great-great grandfather had also been a white boy but he had been born at home in a distant backwater on the opposite side of the Atlantic Ocean, a place from which he had fled one sort of tyranny or persecution or another to arrive in this country where he avoided further persecution, wars or trouble of any kind if you don't count a minor run-in with the authorities over the manufacture and distribution of an illegal beverage.

 Young Jeremy grew to adulthood without ever having heard a word about his great-great-great grandfather, and even to this day does not know that his name had been Joseph Kantheiler, because Joseph Kantheiler, wishing to cut all ties with and reminders of his troubled homeland, had changed the family name to Manson, a name he had copied from the side of a box of fruit shipped from the West Indies. Joseph Manson then married a white girl who had been born in the back of a wagon in some other far-off land and Jeremy didn't know anything about her either.

 Jeremy did learn something of his great-great grandfather, Jeb Manson, who had not been so lucky in avoiding trouble. Jeb, due to the unfortunate timing of his tenure on the planet, found himself caught up in a great Civil War. Jeremy didn't know a lot of other particulars, such as the fact that one of the battles his great-great grandfather participated in, was so fierce that over its three day course, more of Jeb and Jeremy's own countrymen had perished there than in the entire painful episode of Vietnam. Jeremy knows only a little about Vietnam. Some of what he thinks he knows is wrong. He thinks for instance, that Vietnam is in the southern hemisphere. Jeremy, of course lives in a time of short memories and reality TV programs.

 Jeremy still has never been to the venerated battlefield where his great-great grandfather, who came through that engagement without a scratch, leaned against his overheated battery, surrounded by all those poor dead and dying men of his own country. If his great-great grandfather could stand in that very spot now he would be surprised to see that it is little changed from that hot July day—except for the absence of billowing black smoke and the groans of the wounded. Given the passage of time, perhaps he would not be surprised at the muffled roar of not too distant motorized traffic and the red and white roof of a Kentucky Fried Chicken Franchise rising just beyond the ridge from which the suicidal order had been given to charge, straight into the teeth of his fire-breathing cannon.

 Jeremy grew to young adulthood with other white children in a subdivision to which his parents had fled the multi-cultured and dangerous city center. He went to college not far from his home in order to join a fraternity, meet a nice white girl and make some acquaintances, which would serve him well later in life. He got a good-paying job doing unchallenging work for the father of the white girl he met in his English 101 class and married at the age of twenty-five. They had a white boy of their own about two years after their wedding, when Jeremy felt that the time was right.

 Jeremy's blonde wife, Jennifer, thought that it would not be right for the boy, Jarred, and the girl, Jennel, whose birth they had planned for five years hence, to grow up in a home without pets, so they drove to the pound one Saturday morning before the football games came on, and selected a mixed-breed puppy.

 It was white—mostly.

 Jeremy and Jennifer purchased a small house in a new subdivision south of the town they had both grown up in, although they had not known each other previously because they had gone to different high schools. They were not at all surprised that they had met at the college which was 150 miles from their own homes rather than in their own town because Jeremy's subdivision was on the east side of town and Jennifer's subdivision was on the west side of town. Nor were they surprised to have gravitated toward one another because it was the custom of their race to seek out its own kind, and not only were they from the same town, fair of skin and blue of eye, but most said they looked so much alike that they could be brother and sister. They, of course didn't know it, but were in fact distantly related. Jeremy's great-great grandfather had been treated for the wounds he received in a later, smaller battle in which the casualties were only slightly more than the combined totals of all those suffered by his countrymen in Iraq one and two, and the invasion of Granada, by a nurse with whom he had a brief liaison, resulting in a child whom the nurse never let on, did not share her husband's genes. That child turned out to be Jennifer's great-great grandmother.

Anyway, with some financial aid from Jennifer's father, Jeremy and Jennifer moved into their new home with Jarred and their new puppy, Jeffrey. Their subdivision was just like the treeless subdivisions they had each grown up in, so they felt immediately at home. Only three years earlier it had been part of a lovely farm with rolling hills and copses of trees. A very minor Civil War battle had been fought there, and because of that, it had at one time been considered sacred ground. Jeremy remembered driving past the area with his father—now dead—who had pointed out to him the fence, behind which, union soldiers had taken a rather poorly sheltered position with the advantage of high ground—and the cornfield, where ragged confederates had been mowed down along with the stalks.

Neither Jeremy's father, nor the soldiers who had squared off on that farmland had ever given a second thought to the fact that before any of them ever laid eyes on that property it had been a sacred hunting ground of the native peoples who had been displaced from it. Jeremy

Battlefield

knew enough to not refer to those people, if it ever came up in conversation, as Indians. He called them Native Americans in the same way he had learned to call Negroes Black Americans, even the ones who were visiting his country as students at the University he had attended, who were actually Black Africans. The white folks who had appropriated that land the first time, had been kind enough though, to ship the natives off to another place they could call their own, until other white folks, upon discovering their predecessors' mistake, realized that the new place had gold or uranium or oil or some such thing of value lurking under its sage and scrub surface. Then they were sometimes compelled, if the Native Americans who hadn't already died on the long march to the new land they had been awarded, showed any reluctance to comply with this new request, to persuade them by means of violence, to ship off to some new locale. But that's a whole different story altogether.

When Jeremy first noticed bulldozers and other pieces of large yellow machinery scraping away the fields and fences of that consecrated ground and when he saw a sign erected that told of the future site of the Battleground Subdivision and Golf Community, he laid his money down. Some folks were upset that businessmen and developers had secretly shaken hands over this deal which laid waste to a national treasure, but city council members, who were 98 % businessmen and developers themselves, had no problems with such intensions and were more than happy to allow the scraping and digging to commence right away, so that if some tree-hugging, history-buff types raised a stink it would be essentially too late to do anything about it anyway.

Jeremy, who worked for Jennifer's dad who was himself a businessman and developer, pictured in his mind the cozy brick house with two-car garage and concrete driveway, and the two Bradford Pears that would replace the thicket of locust trees the yellow bulldozers had scoured from the site of the skirmish. He was happy to settle in on his little slice of history and he didn't mind that it was also convenient to the interstate highway and shopping. He had never had the time for golf, but living on the Battlefield Golf Course offered just the opportunity to correct that omission from his vitae.

Each evening at around seven, Jeremy and Jennifer took Jeffrey, on his leash and Jarred, in his stroller, for a walk through the subdivision where they would wave at the other white people who might be out watering their lawns or spraying chemicals. Most folks though were inside, watching reality TV in air-conditioned comfort. It gave the young family a pleasant feeling to see the flicker of cathode ray tubes inside the homes just like the one they lived in.

Jeremy was glad that their subdivision had restrictions. You *did* have two choices of brick and two choices of roofing shingles but the trim was all 'clay.' He couldn't help feeling that the union soldiers, the victors in the small skirmish, would have felt vindicated, seeing what had finally been accomplished here.

On his way home from work one day Jeremy noticed that in the yards of some of the older houses, a few miles from the brick and faux stone entrance to Battlefield, there were some dark-skinned children out playing under the big trees They were not black but they were very dark; he suspected that they were from Mexico or Guatemala—one of these Central American countries. When he got home he commented on his observation to Jennifer who said, "Hmm."

They would have redoubled their efforts to lock their doors when they went out or when it was time for bed, but they already did this anyway. That's why on Sunday upon arriving home from church, when they unlocked the doors and stepped inside, they were surprised

Battlefield

to find that the door of their new stainless steel refrigerator had been dented.

Jeremy reported the discovery to the police who sent out a young female officer. She took notes and viewed the damage.

"Are you going to dust for prints?" Jeremy asked.

"I don't think we'd find anything," the young officer said. "Besides, there is no sign of forcible entry. And all the windows are locked."

But Jeremy and Jennifer insisted and the cop called for a team of investigators.

"She's calling in back-up," Jeremy whispered to his wife.

The investigators arrived and made a mess with their muddy shoes and dirty fingerprint kit. It took hours for Jennifer to properly clean the fine black powder from marble countertops and hardwood floors where the cops carelessly tracked the stuff through the house. The investigators found prints belonging to Jeremy, Jarred and Jennifer.

The original officer filed her report, and an abbreviated account of the incident appeared in the local paper in the 'crime beat' section.

Refrigerator dented … was the lead-in to the description of the affair at 337 Gary Player Lane.

Jeremy bought a gun.

It wasn't long before dark-skinned, mustached men could be found in Battlefield Subdivision, cutting grass, and blowing leaves. The white people inside the houses were seldom seen out on their big lawns after the Bradford Pears grew to respectable sizes. The dark-skinned workers enabled them to spend more time watching their new TVs, which were now plasma replacements of the older tube models. Some of the houses, even Jeremy's and Jennifer's—once Jennel came along—had brown-skinned women inside, taking care of the white children when the parents went to jobs, or movies, or shopping. But somehow, after the denting of the refrigerator, no one in the subdivision felt as secure as they had all those years ago when the rolling hills were newly shaved clean of locust trees. The subdivision, with the addition of phases three and four, grew to an immense size and all the white people bought guns, most, bigger than Jeremy's. But Jeremy was not to be outdone and bought himself a bigger gun that was also semi-automatic.

    One day little Jarred found the gun and playfully shot his little sister, Jennel dead.

    The family never did get around to repairing or replacing their refrigerator. Jeremy never got around to taking Jarred or Jennifer to visit the great battlefield with the Kentucky Fried Chicken Franchise located so conveniently nearby.

    The firepower in the subdivision, ironically some say, had increased at the time Jarred blew his little sister's head off, to dwarf that of the long-ago Civil War skirmish that had taken place there.

    One of the officers, who came to investigate the accidental shooting, was the same young woman who had taken the report of the denting so many years before. She had changed very little, Jeremy thought, except for putting on a few pounds. But then who hadn't?

Lakeview Motel   9

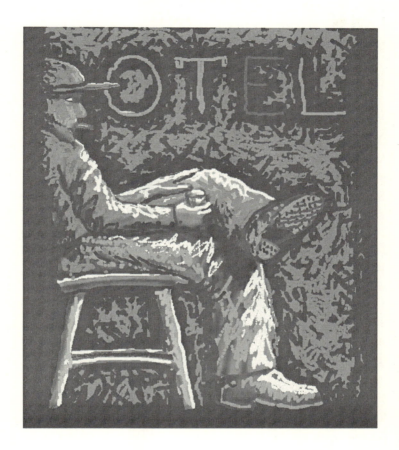

Lakeview Motel

My ass itches like crazy. When I stand on the edge of the tub I can see it in the mirror. And if I look out the window from here—the window is too high to see out otherwise—I can make out a sort of depression that's probably a dried up lakebed. I'm thinking that's why they call it the Lakeview Motel. I guess there used to be a lake here. I like to work these things out in my head. They probably never changed the name because Dried-up Lakebed Motel is a mouthful. It's easy when you're somewhere like in the

Ozarks and it's the Lake of the Ozark's Motel or you're in Illinois and it's the Lincoln Inn. Lincoln was born somewhere in Illinois I guess, or he lived there. Something.

 From up here on the tub, I can see not only the dried lakebed, but there's also a splendid view of this big red rash which is the real reason I up here anyway. Actually now that I think about it, it itches in the front too. Yep, it's all red there too. The rash is exactly the shape of my underwear. What I'd really like to do is start scratching the hell out of it. There's hardly anything better than scratching at something that itches like this. Brenda says that only makes it worse. She's a nurse and so she knows all this stuff about rashes. But since she made me move out, she's not a real big help. I bet she'd have some kind of crap that you put on it, or maybe she could get me a shot. I was always trying to talk her into bringing home some new meds for us to try out. She did once and we got high for a whole weekend on that stuff, but that was a long time ago, when she used to be a lot more fun. She said she'd get in big trouble if she ever did it again and got caught.

 Man, that's discipline. No way I could go all those years knowing that stuff's like right there for the taking and not get into it at least once in a while—like on special occasions—say on your birthday or Easter or something. Our kid, Evan, takes some stuff for these allergies he has. I used to snitch some now and then but it was just those little kid doses. I'd get a little sleepy from it is all.

 There's a guy two doors down from me's got a little dope that he doesn't mind sharing. Last night we sat out until about midnight, shoot'n the shit and smokin' till some bitch upstairs called the cops cause we were makin'n too much noise.

 Me and Cartel—that's the guy's name—Cartel, we got a pretty good look at her. Not too bad. She came out in her bathrobe and leaned over the railing. If I tilted my

Lakeview Motel

head to the left I got a nice titty shot on her. They're these really big balloony ones that look real comfortable—like you could sort of smother yourself in them. We haven't figured out what she's doing here. This place is mostly full of guys that don't have a lot of cash to spare. They work around here in construction or something, so they rent rooms by the week, or else, like Cartel and me, their old ladies gave 'em the boot for one thing or another.

She's got some little kid with her. Yesterday the school bus stopped here and let him out. She seems like one of these pretty good mothers 'cause she came out to the bus to meet him. I could hear her asking stuff like 'how was your day, and did you get a good grade on some test?' Stuff like that.

Reason I'm here at the Lakeview is mostly because Brenda found out about Wendy. Wendy works at this bar I used to go to after I used to get off work at the job I used to have. I tried to tell her, Brenda I mean, that it wasn't a big deal but she got her feathers all ruffled. She was already kinda pissed anyway after I quit my job. But I worked at that place for nearly seven months. Hell, you can't stay in one place forever. Besides, my talents were never appreciated.

I was always putting suggestions in the box, like give us longer smoke breaks and how that would boost morale and so forth. I worked my ass off on those suggestions, but mine never got picked. They took Bud Simpson's though. His was about turning in guys who weren't doing their fair share or were cutting corners on quality ... stuff like that. He got two big bonuses ... one for his suggestion and another for turning *me* in.

Man, this itching is killin' me.

This place isn't so bad really. You got your TV. You got cable. Gets about a hundred stations. They're not the best ones, but they get a couple of those soft porn channels. They're all right even though they cut off all the really good stuff.

Lots of tits, no dicks.

Got me one of those little refrigerators—just big enough to keep beer in really, but I ran out yesterday. Cartel's just about convinced me to switch to bourbon or gin. Brenda, of course says I drink too much. That's one of her reasons for givin' me the old heave-ho. She says I need to get it under control. Now, I've always been real careful to wait until afternoon before I start up, like at least one thirty or two, then I go as slow as I can so I'm not all violent and shit. I usually don't get to my twelfth until just about bed-time. When I say violent I don't mean that I take it out on Brenda or the kid. I just break a lot of stuff. She claims that I hit her a couple of times but I sure don't remember *that*. That's not something you'd be likely to forget.

But anyhoo, the way Cartel sees it, once you start drinking beer, you always drink about twelve or so. He says that by switching to gin he gets a better buzz without having to drink as much as he does with beer. He just sips at it all day. That because gin, and I guess bourbon too, is stronger—like more potent than beer—you know, in the alcohol department. He figures also that drinking less of the actual liquid keeps the weight problem in check. Cartel says he's lost about ten pounds since he switched and he wants me to try it too. I'm kinda overweight and wouldn't mind losing a few.

Actually, last night while we were sitting around, mostly smoking his dope, we got a pretty good idea for makin' a buck or two. He's going to keep—like a chart—on him and me and watch how much weight we drop by switching to gin or bourbon. He's been doing this in his own case and he says that I will be in the 'sample' group.

Course, I don't exactly see myself as a group, so I asked him who else is included his little experiment and he says he's going to see if the bitch upstairs who turned us in wants to join us.

The weight I lose will be reported in our 'findings.' Then we'll put together all our 'findings' into this book. There's these guys, Cartel says, that come up with one kind of diet or another and lot's of people buy in. He says if your book gets to be on the New York Times bestseller list that all your troubles are over because you get a cut on every book they sell. I figure I'm going to get in on *this* action. It sounds a hell of a lot easier than winning that lottery. I've been working on that for years now and the best I've been able to do was this one time I won a thousand bucks on the pick three. I hate to even add up all the dough I spent to get that thousand. And then—I had to use all of it to pay some fine anyway. They said I was doin' like seventy or so in a thirty-five zone and they smelled alcohol—the whole deal.

Anyway, in this one guy's diet, Cartel says, you eat anything you want. That's it—you eat anything you want—you lose weight. And a whole bunch of people bought that book and now that guy's rich. Can you believe that? He even built this place up in the mountains where people pay to come there and listen to him give lectures and stuff and eat all kinds of shit. I told Cartel that I liked that idea a lot. I'm pretty good at talking, see, so I'm pushin' for him to let me do all the lectures—but he says he wants that part. He says that a lot of times when you give these talks it gets the women real turned on by your 'expertise' and all, and they become sort of like your groupies and you get to fuck 'em. But to tell you the truth I'm not all that fired up about the idea of sex with fat bitches anyway. In fact, the thought makes me sorta sick. But it could be OK I guess if they could hold off until they get the weight down some.

Hold the phone. Here's Brenda pullin' into the lot. She's going into the office. Probably talking to the guy in there about me—like am I causing problems and such. She's getting back into her car. Here she comes.

"Hey," I say, opening the door for her. It's bright out and the light hurts my eyes. I don't usually open up until the sun goes behind the billboard across the street.

"Hey," she says back to me.

"Come on in. I'd offer you something but I don't have anything right now."

"That's Ok," she says. "Listen, we need to talk."

"Sure, but hey, could you help me out with something? My ass is killin' me. I got this rash and it itches like hell."

She just looks at me.

"Come on, you see asses all the time and you've seen mine plenty. Maybe you can figure out something I can do."

"All right. Take your pants down. Let me take a look."

I pull my pants down and show her.

"Jesus!" she says. "It's the exact outline of your underwear. It's probably an allergy. Have you changed your detergent?"

"Yeah well, I guess. It's just whatever you get in those little boxes at the Laundromat."

"Well, which one was it, like Tide or All or something?"

"I don't know. I just put in my quarters and take whatever falls out."

"You need to keep track and switch to whatever it isn't."

"Now that I come to think of it," I say, " I'm getting a mental picture of the machine and I think it's the same stuff in each one of the slots. But anyway, can't you get me something to put on it, like some powder or cream or something, or even a shot? Maybe you could bring me something from the hospital. And I've got pain. I could use something for the pain, like you got that one time."

I know I'm pushing my luck here.

"Put your pants back on," she says, turning away. She can tell I'm starting to get a little excited. She still looks pretty good and the memories of our little experience with the pain meds she brought home that time get me kinda worked up.

"Listen, I'm talking to a lawyer. You probably ought to get yourself one. And you should know, there will be some money involved. I'm going to ask for child support. I'm not pressing for anything else, but you've got to kick in. You're going to need to get yourself straightened out and get a job."

Our kid, Evan, he's about the same age as the little kid that gets dropped off by the bus for the woman on the second floor. Shit. I know how these child-support things go. You gotta keep paying until the kid is eighteen or something. That's like—let's see—fourteen years. And if you slip up they send you to jail.

"I got something going," I tell her. "Me and this guy a couple doors down got a little business thing cooked up. He thinks it could be big. I can't really tell you about it yet, but I'll just say this. Keep your eye on the New York Times best seller list."

"I gotta go," she says. "I just wanted to tell you that you need to be looking for a job."

"OK, well … what about my ass, honey? This is really bad. I can hardly sit down."

"I'll see what I can do. I'll bring you something for it tomorrow."

"Ok. Well, see if you can get me something for the pain too. I've got a lot of pain here."

She's not too encouraging about the pain meds but she gives me a little kiss on the cheek.

"Oh, yeah, and one more thing," I say, "I'm a little short. Do you think you could spare a little, just till me and the guy I'm goin' in with get our first royalty check?"

Cartel says that's what our money will be called ... *royalty*. I kinda like saying that to Brenda 'cause it sounds impressive. I'm guessing she's buyin' it 'cause she forks over a twenty.

When she gets back in her car, I can see that there's some guy in it, waiting for her. I didn't see him when she drove up because it was so bright out and my eyes weren't adjusted, but the sun's gone behind the billboard now and I can see better. He looks like one of these real dull types, coat and tie and all. He's reading some book. Who knows? Maybe he'll be one of our customers, Cartel and me.

I head out to the liquor store to get some bourbon. I'll share it with Cartel later on and we can get started on our book. I'm really kind of excited about this. And if I can get my nerve up I'm going to talk to the lady up on the second floor. I might see if she wants to get in on our deal, not a full partner but we can cut her in for some kind of percentage maybe, if Cartel agrees. Besides, I wouldn't mind getting a closer look at those tits before the kid gets home.

Summit Fever

Since my return, I've scuttled around in the dark like a cockroach ... in rooms with shades drawn, or mid-afternoon movie theatres. It was Kara who initiated contact—who forced me out into the open.

I'm glad she chose this dimly lit bar where I can

shield my sun-scorched eyes from the world a bit longer. I can picture Peter, the way he looked the day I first saw him. It was in the Tetons. Taylor, my so-called boyfriend had gone on, leaving me there at 10'000 feet with a splitting headache for hours. It was embarrassing, sitting there while climbers and hikers passed on their way up or down, asking if I was all right. When Peter came along, he sat down and waited with me, a total stranger.

"Everything OK here?" he asked.

"Sure," I said. "I was feeling a bit woozy so I decided to stay here while my friend went on. I'll be fine."

Peter aborted his chance to go on to the top of Grand Teton, just to hang there with me until Taylor came back down. He shared his water and trail mix. He gave me his number. It was a few weeks later, when I realized what a shit Taylor was—it took catching him with my best friend to cinch it—that I called Peter. I didn't know if he'd remember me but he said, "Greta, sure ... let's eat."

When Kara's lean shape appeared against the backlight of the open door, it could have been her brother's—that same confident stride, the same self-assured physicality that would lend a sense of well being to anyone within shouting distance, even in the face of extreme conditions.

I stand to greet her.

"Greta," she says, taking both my hands. "How are you? I'm so sorry."

"Me too," I say fighting back tears. "It must be tough on you too. How ... how are your parents holding up? I got a card ... but ..."

Kara waves a dismissive hand but after a pause she says, "It's hard. The stories ... in the paper ... and ... the descriptions. It's all a bit too much for them right now. They *want* to see you, but it's not time yet. I'm sorry but it'll take awhile. They'll come around though. We're tough ...our family. We ..."

Summit Fever

She stops talking and releases my hands as the waitress arrives. Kara orders a glass of white wine.

"So, I don't suppose there's any other topic you'd like to talk about," I say.

She gives short, polite laugh.

"No. I need to know. I need to know everything. I thought you were against the expedition from the start. He hadn't even told us you'd be going."

"Ok, well, let me start from the beginning."

"Fine."

"You remember the summer we met."

"Out west, right?" she says.

"Right."

We review together the details of our meeting in Wyoming and the following summer in Colorado where he gradually helped me build my stamina to the point where I did three fourteeners with him, Culebra, Holy Cross, and Handies.

"We got buckshot fired at us on the trail to Culebra 'cause it's on private land."

"Yeah," Kara smiles, "I remember him telling us about that," she says.

"He first started working on me to go with him to a *big* mountain, 8000 meters, there on top of Culebra Peak, a gentle hill really. I guess he thought I'd be eager to up the ante, but at the time, I was happy just aiming for Mt. Sneffels in August.

Then Doug asked him to join them at Kangchenjunga. After that there was …" I count them on my fingers, "Nanga Parbat, the winter attempt on Gasherbrum II … Annapurna I, then Malaku. Peter had been on two previous 8000 meter climbs when we met. I had never been above 14,000 feet, when he convinced me to go with him to Malaku … as far as base. I had a few headaches and lost twenty pounds, but I was much stronger than I thought I'd be."

"Who couldn't lose twenty pounds?" Kara says.

"Right. Anyway, since I was able to do that much, he somehow talked me into doing *this* climb with him."

"What did the rest of the guys think? I know how they usually feel novices."

"I'm sure they weren't thrilled with the idea, but he guaranteed them that I would be his responsibility. Also, he said he wouldn't go without me. Anyway, once we were on the mountain, I did my share. I helped fix ropes and placed ladders. I didn't whine or get too many headaches and more importantly, didn't cause any. I think they accepted me as one of the team. He had promised me that everyone would be on oxygen. No tough-guy stuff."

"Ok," Kara says. "So you're on the mountain."

"Well, not quite. The trek in to base takes eight days. Then two weeks of acclimatization—trips up and down the glacier and the northeast ridge cutting steps. That was when I found out he had lied to me."

"Lied?"

"Yeah, about the oxygen. He had no intention of using oxygen. He told me that so I'd agree to come. He wanted *me* to use it of course, but something happens to you once you're actually on the mountain. Your pride kicks in. I figured if he wasn't using it, then by god, neither was I. It was hard at first but as we worked our way up to, around 24,000, I got stronger and stronger. Some days we did 5,000 feet or more then returned all the way to base. We'd stay at base for two days before going back up. You know ... climb high, sleep low."

As we talk, two guys at a table in the corner send us drinks.

"Oh great," Kara says. We nod our thanks in a way that we hope indicates politeness without interest and turn back toward each other in what could only be construed as a gesture of discouragement.

"There were three other teams on the mountain," I

continue, "the Japanese women, a team from *Outside* magazine and the Russians who were ascending from the Chinese side. But we had to make the highest of the high camps because our ridge only offered one protected point. The day we made the push to 25,000 where we would set up our final camp, something happened to me. It was warm that day and Peter was worried about avalanches. I was walking slower and slower. He was leading and he kept waiting for me to catch up. He wanted to get out of the gully we were in before a big one broke loose, but I remember becoming fascinated with my arms. I could hardly move because I was so interested in watching them detach themselves from my body and float away. I tried to show Peter. I wanted him to see it. His arms were just the same as always but mine were so beautiful, floating like that.

Then I began to worry that I would bleed to death with my arms gone. That's when he put me on oxygen and my arms came back. We went back down to base where I recuperated over a two-day period. But that was an awakening. That's the kind of thing the altitude can do to your judgment when it hits you."

One of the guys who sent us the drinks, comes over to our table.

"Hi there," he says, "I'm Dave and my friend at the over there," He nods in Arnie's direction. "That's Arnie."

Arnie lifts his beer mug in a drunken salute.
"We ..."

"Listen," I say, taking note of the tan line on Dave's wedding ring finger, "thanks for the drinks. That was very nice of you but we just came here to talk. OK? We don't get to see each other very often."

Dave looks only mildly crushed. He raises a hand as if to say 'sorry' and returns to his pal who droops like a dog realizing he's not included in the ride in the car-car.

"So, you decided to go back on oxygen?" Kara says.

"No. I felt fine after a few days and I was ready to go back up, but during that time a storm hit. It lasted for four days. We heard that the Russian team got trapped high up and lost a climber. Then one of the Japanese women died from pulmonary edema. I saw her when they brought her down. Naturally when you see that you think, 'that could be me.' But that doesn't last long. You've come that far and the thought of turning back is pretty distasteful. The Japanese team left the mountain and so did the Russians. The *Outside* guys had helped in what they thought was to be a rescue of the Japanese but it turned out to be a recovery effort. I guess that left them pretty bummed because they gave it up too after the next storm swept through. Randal and Jeff from our team were caught up at five in that one. They were planning to summit the morning it hit. They had to bivouac and by the time they got back to base, Randal was snow-blind and Jeff had frostbitten fingers and toes. So naturally they were ready to leave as well. But Peter and I wanted to wait at least one more day to see if it cleared. We felt very strong and if the weather allowed, we wanted our shot. The others agreed in the end, that after all our hard work, we deserved our chance.

We awoke to a perfect morning. We could see the top clearly. In that crystal air it seemed that you could reach out and touch it. So we got the go-ahead and Peter and I set out to make the high camp. It took twelve hours but we arrived in good condition. There were two oxygen tanks in the tent and Peter insisted that I sleep with one. I didn't fight him on that. I figured that *climbing* without it would be good enough for me."

"So you were both fine at that point?" Kara asked. "The night before the summit bid."

"I felt great. Peter complained of a slight headache

but no one would have thought that was unusual. The plan was to leave at 1:00 AM. There was a three quarter moon and we barely needed our lamps. For most of the way I had Peter in sight. He was definitely not climbing at his usual pace but that was fine with me. I was roped to him of course, on a long lead. I felt strong—no hallucinations this time. The weather was deteriorating below but up ahead things still looked good.

We were going to make it.

When we stopped for a brief rest he complained that his head was still hurting. I asked him if it was serious enough that we should turn back but he waved that idea off. I really didn't think much more of it. I remember singing to myself, at a very slow beat, *'When I'm Sixty-four.'* I would keep time with my footfalls, which I found funny because the line ... *when I get older, losing my hair...* took almost a minute by my watch. I was lost in my own thoughts and determined not to look up because I didn't want to keep thinking how much farther it was. I just wanted to suddenly be there. But at some point I did look up—and I didn't see Peter."

"So you don't know what happened?"

I knew this would be the difficult part. But it was time someone knew the whole story. Kara seemed strong enough to hear the truth.

I place a hand on her arm.

" I saw that the rope had gone slack but still trailed up the ridge. I went on ... calling for him all the way. No answer. When I crossed a little rise I saw something red lying in the snow. When I got to him, I could tell he was in real trouble, probably cerebral edema. He was breathing, but barely. His eyes were wide open and his pupils were dilated. There was nothing that could have been done. He was dead.

He was still alive ... but he was dead."

"But," Kara says, "I thought ... I thought they

never ... found him."

"We were above 28,000 feet. It's all you can do at that altitude to drag your own feet an inch or two at a time."

"What about your oxygen? Couldn't you have given him some of yours?"

"Didn't have it—not with me. We had agreed that I didn't need it. We both felt strong and you can move faster without the tanks. There was a full canister back at the high camp, but that was five hours below us. You've got to understand. It was impossible. Besides, even if I had oxygen, it wouldn't have done any good. His brain was swollen. The only thing you can do is get down ...way down ...fast or get into a decompression bubble. Even base camp would have been too high."

"What *about* base? Why didn't they try to do something?"

"I didn't tell them."

Kara pulls her hand away with a look of horror.

"I'll never tell them. There was nothing they could have done. I hope you won't tell anyone either. What's the point of more people feeling responsible? The last they had heard from him indicated that we were fine. We were near the top. You've got to understand. If I had told them, it wouldn't have made any difference to the outcome. Weather was beginning to move in from below. If they had started up, they would have been caught in the storm. They were already injured themselves. There *is* no rescue from that altitude. It would be impossible for anyone to carry him down. I couldn't have done it even it if we only been at 8,000 feet. He was going to be dead in minutes. Even if something could have been done for him, he didn't have the hours it would have taken in the best of conditions, for them to reach him. Would you have risked their lives in a hopeless cause? Peter—everyone who goes up there—knows what they are getting themselves into."

Kara continues to stare at me accusingly.

"He said to me once, there's a mental trick to getting to the top. Once you get the hang of it, it's easy. You can't *mind* if you don't come back."

"So you just left him there?" Kara says. "He's still lying on that ridge where others will pass by and gawk at his dead body?"

"Let me finish." I take a sip of my beer to compose myself. "I had to get moving. Looking at him, I knew that if I didn't get going, that would be me lying there soon. When I looked down toward the tents we had left that morning they were just tiny dots. The clouds hadn't reached our high camp yet but they were boiling up toward it. Base must have been in the thick of the storm at that point. I looked up and it was clear up there and—so close—not more than three hundred feet to go."

"You went on to the summit?"

"What would Peter have done? A month on the mountain and three hundred feet to go. This was *it* for me—my one shot. I'll never be back there."

"You must not have been thinking clearly," Kara says, that look of incredulity still on her face. "You were oxygen deprived."

"Everything was clear. I did what I did."

It was true that my thought processes may have been clouded. But I knew that it wasn't the lack of oxygen. It was the mountain itself. I had the fever. It was the magnetic pull of the summit that wouldn't release me, even if all my rationalization about Peter's condition was absolutely true ... and it was. The real question I am still wrestling with is ... what would I have done if he *hadn't* been dying? Would the attaction of the summit still have pulled me upward, leaving him to fend for himself?

I pull a packet of photos from my jacket and hand them to her. She thumbs through them—pictures of Peter and me, a group photo of the Japanese women standing under a string of prayer flags, views of the endless peaks poking their glossy summits above a sea of gray clouds, all of them below the point from which the picture had been taken. She lingers for a while at the time-delay self-portrait—my smiling face next to the flags and ice axes that constitute the makeshift marker designating the summit.

She hands the photos back to me, turning her face away from mine.

"Peter warned me many times," I say, looking down into my empty beer mug. "Most people who die, die on the way down. I descended carefully, watching each step as if it could be my last. The ridge dropped away on either side for thousands of feet. When I got to where I had left him ... he was gone."

Kara turns her bitter face back to me but says nothing.

"I saw drag marks heading downward, but they disappeared over the edge. I got as close as I dared; then I saw him. I'm sure he was dead. He ... his rope had caught in some rocks. He was hanging ... seven-thousand feet above the glacier."

There is a long silence between us now. She stares at me.

"I couldn't just leave him like that."

She turns away from me again. After a pause she says softly, "You cut the rope."

I don't answer.

Without another word, she lays some money on the table and walks out of the bar. She doesn't look back.

I sit there for a while. The waitress reappears and I order another beer and send one over to Dave and Arnie. I sip at my fresh beer as I review my photos from the top of the world.

Dave saunters over my way.

Scumbag

Scumbag

"So, are you still fucking her?"
    Oh, man. Here we go again. All eyes are on me. This is one tough question. I haven't seen my wife, Marjorie in nearly two months? Surely other events are more important in the big picture than this question of hers. Tutsis are butchering Hutus. Arabs are blowing up

Jews or anybody else who gets in their way. Hurricanes have trashed Florida—and my neighbor, James Pettigrew—had a heart attack trying to make it from his car to his front door in a thunderstorm without getting hit by lightning. About a minute later, lightning struck his Bradford Pear, splitting it down the middle. Its halves fell on either side of him like God making some kind of parenthetical statement.

But Marjorie's still all bent out of shape about me fucking her sister.

I had expected the issue to hover in the air over our meeting, but I hadn't expected it to be so audible. I look to my lawyer, Stephanie Boardman for guidance. I assume Stephanie has heard such language before, perhaps in this very conference room, because her face registers no shock.

Stephanie's all prim and proper looking in those little round glasses and that suit, but I bet she's hot underneath all that. She'd probably loosen up a bit—if I could get a drink or two down her. I try to picture her with that hair down spilling over a pillow.

I should say something but I find myself at a loss for words. Marjorie, Stephanie, Marjorie's lawyer Binford McLeash—they all wait for something in the way of a response from me but I remain silent until at last the words, "citizen's arrest" spoken with the hick accent of Gomer Pyle, are the ones I come up with. I had been watching an old episode of the Andy Griffith show on the TV in the waiting room.

"Citizen's arrest." I say again. Everyone glares at me. Their eyes remind me of James Pettigrew's lifeless stare. I didn't see him right away. I had gone out to gawk at his lightning-divided Bradford Pear. It was only when I heard the ding-ding from his open car door that I spotted him, flat on his back, between the bushy halves of his weak ornamental tree.

"Perhaps we should proceed," Stephanie suggested.

Scumbag

The two lawyers begin pulling papers from their briefcases.

"Citizen's arrest."

This time I mouth the words silently across the table to my soon-to-be-ex-wife who stares back at me coldly. She's so bitter, just because I fucked her kid sister a few times. What about me? I was just supposed to take it when she started messing around with my boss Sidney Terrible ... who is a Democrat, by the way. How can you do that with a Democrat and still live with yourself?

As the lawyers read the divorce agreement, supposedly an amicable separation document, I pretend to be listening with interest. Marjorie keeps her eyes down, tracing some spot on the table with her finger. Me, I'm thinking about the power *fucking* holds over us. How did this happen? Everybody fucks. It's part of nature. Everybody goes to the bathroom, everybody sleeps—everybody fucks. Animals do it all the time and they don't get all upset over it and go telling all their furry friends or calling lawyers.

The lawyers are going over the details of the decree now—how much money I will have to give her, who gets the house, when visits with the children will take place—where—who picks them up, how many times a month, how much I will send her to provide them with food, clothing and shelter.

These are all just numbers and times that really don't have any meaning since Sidney Terrible fired me. I don't really have this money they're all talking about anyway. I sign the meaningless document as though I will somehow be able to come up with the dough.

Marjorie is keeping the car so, picking the kids up is just a figure of speech as well. I don't really have anyplace to live. So even if I can work out a way for Marjorie to drop them off, I don't know where we would go for a whole weekend. I like to sit and write in the park on the south side of town. I guess they could run around there until dark. Park security always shoos me away then. I'm working on a spy-novel. I still have my laptop but I haven't seen it for a while. I keep retracing my steps but I can't remember where I left it. It'll probably turn up though, unless it's been stolen.

Suddenly I have a terrible thought. I see myself walk into Barnes and Noble and there's my novel, *Dick Darkley, Secret Agent*, number one on the New York times best seller list. But the author is someone else, the guy who stole my laptop and the manuscript in it.

I'm wondering if Stephanie'd let me crash at her place. I could bring the kids there but I get the feeling she doesn't like kids very much—especially my two brats. I had 'em with me once and they fragmented some stuff in the waiting room. I'm not crazy about 'em either but you're supposed to take care of them whether you like them or not.

It's all part of the parenting deal.

At the close of the meeting, I get up from the table and stumble. I fall flat on my face. Nobody helps me up. They all look kind of embarrassed. They think it's because I had a couple beers before I got here. Stephanie said she could smell it on my breath. Big deal. Marjorie thinks I have a "problem." I guess Sidney thought so too. But they don't know how much I've cut back. I've got that completely under control.

"It's these damned bifocals," I explain. "When I look down it seems like the floor is too close."

We all shake hands and that's pretty much that. I'd like to see if Stephanie wants to meet me for a drink when they're all gone but she seems pretty cold about the whole deal, real business-like and all, so I figure I'll just get going. I walk down First Street to a bar I know. Might as well have one for the road. I put my glasses in my pocket. I don't want to stumble out here in the street.

Sidney Terrible.

I wonder if he made that up.

I call Marjorie's sister from the bar. She works at the library.

"Hey, Jennifer" I say. "It's me. I was wondering if I could see you tonight. Maybe we could have dinner."

There's a long pause.

"Um ... I don't think that's a good idea. I already have plans."

"Aw come on. I just got out of that divorce meeting thingy, and I'm feeling kind of down. I need to see you."

"I really can't talk now. I'm pretty busy."

"What about tomorrow?"

"I don't think so. Listen, Richard, what happened between us was a big mistake. It's over. You need to get on with your life and let me get on with mine."

"Hell. That's easy for you to say. I lost my marriage, my job. You get off scott-free here."

"Well, I wouldn't say that. You know that what we did ... it was wrong."

I can tell she's sort of crying now. Not out and out sobbing but it's one of those breaky things you can hear in their voice.

"My own sister! I can hardly live with myself. She won't speak to me anymore. I've disappointed my whole family. That's not exactly nothing."

When she hangs up I order another beer. I guess she thinks it's all a big deal too. Just like Marjorie.

Sisters.

When I get ready to leave, I start to lay some cash on the bar. That's when I notice that I have only two bucks in my wallet and some loose change in my pocket. The two dollars will cover my tip; it's the remainder of the bill that is a problem. I put the two bills in the jar and go to the bathroom. There's a guy in one of the stalls and I have to wait through the noises and stink, breathing though my mouth until he finally leaves after an elaborate hand-washing routine. I lock the door and begin prying up the paint-sealed window with my Swiss Army knife. When I get it open I drop painfully into the alley, a story below, tearing my pants on the way down. I sprain my ankle, not badly, but enough that I limp noticeably.

It's raining and I really don't have anywhere to go. I had been counting on Stephanie or Jennifer. I stand under an awning until the rain lets up a bit. As I walk along Third Street, I see a Chevy with its blinkers on, stopped in front of a Copier service. There's nobody in the car. The lights inside are very bright and a guy in a raincoat is standing at the counter discussing business with the girl behind the desk. I watch her walk back to a machine. Nice ass. She begins copying papers. The guy looks back toward the door shielding his eyes against the bright interior lights. He's checking his car, making sure everything is OK with it I guess, since he's left the motor running.

When he turns back to watch the progress of his copies I slip behind the wheel and put the car in drive. He doesn't notice a thing as I slowly drive away. Down the street, I turn the headlights on and tune in my favorite radio station. What luck. On the seat next to me is a cell phone.

Veronica Waters.

I try to remember her home phone number. She was Sidney's secretary at one time. We had a thing a few years back. I try out a few variations, getting wrong numbers. Then, somehow, I pull her cell phone number out of my ass.

"Hello," she says.
"Hey, Veronica, It's me, Richard."
"Richard?"
"Yeah, Rick, Rick Donovan."
"So ... I haven't heard from *you* in a while," she

says. I can hear in her voice that she's intrigued.

"Yeah, well, I haven't been around much. Just got back in town and I thought I'd give you a call, see what you've been up to."

Silence.

"I thought you might want to meet me for a drink or something."

A cop car is headed toward me with its lights flashing. I turn down a dark street as it passes.

"Geez! I don't hear from you for two years and out of the blue, you suddenly get thirsty. Where are you?" she asks.

I look for a street sign.

"I'm downtown. Uh … corner of Ninth and Broadway. Where are you? Sounds like you're driving."

She laughs. "Corner of Ninth and Broadway," she says.
I turn to look over my shoulder, wondering which car she's in.

I guess what they say about the dangers of driving while intoxicated and talking on a cell phone behind the wheel of a stolen car must be true—because at that moment I rear-end Veronica.

"Shit!" I hear her say over the phone. "Some asshole just hit me."

We get out of our cars. She doesn't see me at first as she inspects her bumper for damage. A few people gawk at our little incident.

"What?" I yell at this one guy who just stares at me like he's never seen a drunk before.

She looks up at me.

"Oops," I say.

"Jesus Christ!" she says when she recognizes me.

"Nah, it's just me."

I figure, why lie now?

"Listen. I just stole this car. We need to get out of

here pronto."

I can't believe it. She not only agrees; she seems mildly excited by the whole thing. There is minimal damage to her car. I'm not sure about the Chevy but it's no big deal. People that steal cars are always wrecking them like that. I see that in the paper all the time. I have the presence of mind to grab the guy's cell phone and toss it out Veronica's window as we drive away.

Veronica takes me to this bar on the other side of town from our wreck. By the time we're ready to leave I think she's more looped than me.

"You know what?" I say. " I can't believe it but, I don't have any money on me."

I show her the emptiness of my wallet and she gives me a kind of knowing smile.

"Same as always," she says as she pays the bill.

"I guess I could rob something," I offer.

She laughs. "Everyone says you're a low-life scum bag, but I never thought so, not really."

"Thanks. I'll tell you what we could do," I say. "Let's go break some shit."

I've been telling her about Sidney firing me. She doesn't like the son of a bitch either since he fired her too.

We decide to go over to his house and break out a few of his windows. There's a wall all around his property with a locked gate at the front. I get a tire-iron out of Veronica's trunk. She stays in the car as I climb over and just about tear my pants the rest of the way off. When I get up to the house the windows are too high to get to with the tire iron. In the drive I see my own car, my '98 Corvette. A light comes on and Marjorie walks through a room carrying a drink.

I've got to smash something.

I hate to do it, but I guess after all, it's really not my car anymore.

Scumbag

In the morning, I awake in Veronica's bed. She's in the shower. When she comes out of the bathroom she's wrapped in a towel, drying her hair. She smiles at me. I don't remember much about last night but she seems happy enough.

I peek under the covers and find nakedness.

"So, how'd I do?" I ask.

"Best I've had since Brad Pitt."

I feel sort of proud of myself, although I doubt her Brad Pitt story. Surely I was better than that.

"I've got to go to work," she says. "Make yourself some breakfast. There are eggs and bacon in the fridge or there's cereal in the pantry. I'll be home around five. I'll stop and get bottle of wine and something to cook. I hope you're still here."

She kisses me on the cheek. It's all very domestic.

I pull back the curtain and watch as she backs out of the drive. I fry up some eggs with bacon and whole-wheat toast. I should do the dishes but I don't. I hate doing dishes. I still don't have any money so I start rumaging through drawers. I find a few bucks ... a ten in her underwear drawer and two ones that had fallen behind the refrigerator. I turn over the leather Lazy-Boy in her TV room and some change falls out of it. On a shelf in the living room I pick up a baseball from its little stand. It has signatures all over it and a date ... 1951. The only name I recognize is Bobby Thompson. I remember her telling me that it was her dad's. I know about Thompson's famous home run but it couldn't be *that* ball. That would be worth a lot. Probably in some museum in a glass case or in some big shot's safety deposit box. I turn it over a few times, reading all the names. Never heard of any of the others. This is just one of those deals where the whole team signs the ball. I toss it and it bounces off the wall just like a new one. I put it back on its little stand.

In the bathroom I find her jewelry box. She'd notice the absence of big stuff so I root around until I turn up an old brooch and some clunky looking ring, probably her mom's or something. I'm guessing she won't miss these for a while.

Before I leave the house I call Marcel. I walk a mile or so to a pawnshop, where I turn the two items into 15 bucks. Marcel meets me a couple blocks from the pawnshop. He sells me a nickel bag. I get high on the weed but save some for Veronica. She'll appreciate that. She's gonna get a lot more good out of that ring and brooch than she would have if *I* hadn't turned up. I feel sort of good about myself ... about not being a total prick and all.

When I get back to her house I'm feeling like such a prince that I figure I might as well go all the way and do the dishes. I break a plate when a fucking wasp flies through the window and stings me right in the middle of my forehead. Shit!

I give Jennifer a call down at the library. I can't help myself. I keep thinking about that nice little ass of hers. Veronica's OK but she's gotten a little pudgy since I saw her last. Some guy Jennifer works with picks up. I've talked to him before, Roger or Rudy ... something like that. He says he'll get her, but when he comes back on line he tells me she's not working today. I figure this is probably bullshit and toy with the idea of going down there but I'd have to walk. I guess I'll just stay here and do the rest of the weed with Veronica when she gets home, but before I realize it, it's all gone.

More wasps come in through the window and I decide that since I don't have any more dope to share with her, I should try to do something nice for her. Outside, I find where they're coming from. It's one of those big spiral paper nests that hangs from an insubstantial looking little stalk from the overhang outside her kitchen window. I could knock it down with a stick I bet, but my guess is … that wouldn't end well.

They make this spray stuff that shoots a little stream out and kills the fuckers on contact. I look around under cabinets and in the garage, but all I can come up with is this crap called LOK-EZ that's supposed to thaw out frozen door locks. I test it by spraying a big spider in the garage. Seems to work OK. The spider goes nuts, running around like crazy until he slows down and starts curling up. His legs contract into a ball. Probably burns or something. I spray some on my arm to check it. Yep. Burns the shit out of my arm. After a while it starts to itch so I look around for some bleach. That shit burns too, especially on top of that lock-thaw stuff.

When I get back to the spider, it looks like he's actually getting better. He starts walking again, only real slow, so I stomp on him. I figure this is what will happen to the wasps too. They'll slow down. That'll buy me some time until I can put the rest of my plan into action.

I go shoot some at the nest.

Big mistake.

They're mad as hell now. They start chasing my ass around the yard, with me swatting like a lunatic. I get stung once right where the bleach and LOK-EZ has already got me pretty sore. Finally they give up and go back to the nest where they fly around with all their friends who are also pretty excited. I'm not ready to give up just yet though. I find some more cans of stuff to try out, liquid Pledge and some old spray-paint. I figure I can really slow them down if I get the nest all waterlogged—like. Some of the black paint gets on the nest—more on the house. I wait for them to calm down again and this time I go back to the LOK-EZ and hold my lighter into the stream when I spray it.

Now *this* really works! The stream lights up like a high school fart. A couple of wasps catch on fire and come after me. I shoot more paint at them. They fly back to the nest like little incendiary bombs and before you know it the nest is on fire. I figure now would be a good time for that stick, so I swat at it. I miss, but a bunch of them come for me anyway. It's like all those fighters that come swarming out of the Empire's battle-star after Luke Skywalker. I give up on that. The nest is still hanging on that stalk thing like it's a steel cable or something. Those are pretty tough little structures. The fire spreads from the nest to the eves and soon, I have to admit that we've got a pretty good house-fire under way. This wasn't really what I had in mind. It's getting pretty close to five o'clock, when Veronica said she'd be back. I figure I had better get going. It's true I was trying to do something nice for her but I bet she'll be upset at how it turned out.

    It's not all that far to the library. I might as well head down there and see if that guy—Roger or Rudy—was lying to me about Jennifer. Before I go, I run back in and get the baseball. I might be able to smooth-talk her if I had some more dope to prime the pump with.

Gretchen of Wisconsin 39

Gretchen of Wisconsin

Gretchen descended from Wisconsin, all puffed up on beef and dairy, into the land of the lean, alighting at the Thundercloud Christian Camp, a retreat run by the Baptists high in the Sangre de Christo mountains, to partake of the fellowship of other young crusaders against premarital sex.

Frank Jr. found *his* way to the encampment from his home in Georgia. JR, as he was known to friends and family, was similarly bloated on biscuits, gravy and Peanut

Buster Parfaits. Like Gretchen and all the other young people at the conference, Frank Jr. was a right-wing religious celibacy zealot. These young oath-takers gathered, just outside the tiny ranching community of Sled Lake, to swear off sex—until lawfully wedded to a God-fearing partner of the opposite gender.

Frank Jr. didn't really see the big deal about being *right wing,* a term that seemed to personify evil, according to the television news. As far as he could tell, the values of right-wingers seemed to be the only correct values. But on the night before he was to leave Macon for the retreat, Molly Vann Loo, a local TV news personality, a very pretty, and in Frank Jr.'s opinion—worldly—young woman, had called him a *pawn of the religious right*.

She told him this "off air" because her tone would have been a dead give-away of her attitudes about the religious right, who ran the town, the state, and the TV station she worked for. It was clear to him that she did not approve of him, yet when the lights and camera came to life she had been all smiles.

"And so, Mr. Jackson ..."

"Please call me Junior or JR."

"Yes ... so ... JR, your church is sending you, as a representative of Georgia's youth, to a mission in Colorado. What is it that you and your group of young people wish to accomplish there?"

"We want to tell the world, Miss Vann Loo, that it's OK to be a virgin. It's not something to be ashamed of. Not only is it OK, it's what Jesus would want us to do. I'm not saying, of course, that we should give up sex forever, but in these times of moral decay, ranging from suggestive music to Hollywood mo..."

Frank Jr. saw the director give Molly the slit throat signal. He hurried to finish his statement.

"We are saying—Jesus is saying—that sex should be preserved for the sanctity of marriage. We as

Gretchen of Wisconsin

Christians, should be able to show self-restraint as our Lord would have wished."

After the news, over a pitcher of Heineken down at the G-Spot, Molly and her crew yucked it up about the fat kid who had needlessly sworn off sex.

*

At the camp, Gretchen and Frank Jr. were outsiders. The other young people were mostly wiry, outdoorsy granola types from this fittest of states. Frank and Gretchen definitely stood out from the crowd. Still, everyone was nice enough to them. They were all Christians after all, and as such, went out of their way to show tolerance.

"So is this your first time in Colorado?" asked Jenny, a nice, small town girl from Moffat.

Jenny was petite, blonde, blue-eyed—thin. She looked just like all the other girls Gretchen had seen here.

"Yes. In fact, it's the first time I've been west of the Mississippi."

"I've never been to Mississippi," Jenny said.

So, Gretchen thought, being thin doesn't make you any smarter.

"Well," Jenny said, "the altitude can dehydrate you. So you need to drink lots of water. If not, you'll get like—sick. OK?"

"OK."

Jenny showed Gretchen to her bunk, where instead of drinking water, she ate one of the Snickers bars she had packed along from Wisconsin and got really—like—sick.

The Christian young men Frank Jr. met at the camp, treated him with similar kindness. Even back home in Georgia, where being overweight was not uncommon, he still drew some ribbing for his excesses. Of course, as his friends had advanced into their late teens and early twenties, their own girths were beginning to close the gap on his.

But these guys were nice. They showed him to his bunk and they warned him about the altitude and they told him to drink water and he nodded to indicate that he understood and he ate candy instead—and he got sick too.

*

In the morning, after the devotional and group sing-along, Frank Jr. was the first to speak. It was his job to lay the foundation for the theme of this particular assembly of young believers.

> Believing that true love waits
> I make a commitment to God
> to myself
> to my family
> to my friends
> to my future mate
> and my future children
> to be sexually abstinent
> from this day
> until the day I enter a biblical marriage relationship.

Signed: _____

Date: _____

This was the text of the pledge that Frank Jr. waved before his youthful, like-minded audience.

Enthusiastic cheers met Frank Jr.'s pronouncement. In the audience, Frank saw Gretchen looking back at him with admiration. Amidst the sea of fit, slim, Westerners, the gravitational force of their masses seemed to be pulling them into a mutual orbit. Despite the righteousness of their cause and their moral struggle against human

Gretchen of Wisconsin

weakness, some chemistry stirred their corpulent loins.

Other speakers followed, including Gretchen, who told of pregnancies and disease resulting from this wickedness that she had witnessed first hand at her college in rural Wisconsin. At the end of the day of testimonials, the attendees lined up to sign their pledges and pin their badges, proudly proclaiming their oaths of abstinence.

"Hi," Gretchen said, "I'm Gretchen Olsen." She reached out to shake Frank's hand. "I really enjoyed your talk. It was so sincere and inspirational. And I just adore your accent."

"Thanks," Frank said. "I could do without the accent part though."

"Well, it's just so unusual to hear somebody with a southern accent who seems ..." she fumbled for the right words now, blushing.

"Smart?" Frank suggested. "Or at least not stupid? It's quite a combo," he admitted. "A southern accent and ..." He patted his rotundity with both hands.

"Well," she said, "I'm not exactly a super-model myself."

Over dinner of beef and vegetables, washed down with iced tea, served up by healthy young people with the giant letters STAFF spelled across their shirts, Gretchen and Frank Jr. discussed their interests, their college majors—hers art, at UW Stevens Point, his—music, at Peabody in Nashville, their travels—hers Florida a few times—his Europe, Scotland, Ireland and Wales. They each ate modest portions in an attempt to not appear piggish in front of the other. Gretchen was somewhat uncomfortable with calling him JR as he had asked her to—it seemed so NASCAR.

He was equally uncomfortable with her name, wishing there was some diminutive for "Gretchen." So cold—so northern-sounding and formal.

Over the next two days, the natural order of things

saw a pairing off of newly-met, abstinent couples. Among them were Frank Jr. and Gretchen. During pauses in official conference business, they went for walks along local segments of the lower trail that ran the sixty-mile length of the range. It wound along the drainages at an average elevation of around 9000 feet. The globular pair struggled for breath whenever the path inclined in front of them. But each day it became easier and they ventured further from the camp. Many side trails led off from this artery into the upper lake basins. Most of the lakes lay in alpine valleys between 11,000 and 13,000 feet.

"You want to try the Lake of the Clouds trail?" Frank asked.

"I guess we could start out on it. We can always turn back. Right?"

"Right."

Along the way, other campers and hikers from all over—families with small children, elderly couples with bandaged knees and walking sticks—gained on them and passed them by. At a spot where they could look out over the valley, nowhere near the first lake, they stopped to rest. Frank put his arm around her as they admired the scenery—panting. Gretchen was getting one of the headaches she had been having since her arrival. Sometimes they got so bad they caused her to throw up, especially after she ate, so she had taken to eating very little. Frank noticed that his appetite had also waned. His new friend Richard, from Colorado Springs, told him that loss of appetite was a common side effect of the altitude.

"I think I'm going to have to turn back," Gretchen said.

"Sure, that's OK. I'm getting pretty tired myself. Did you see that old guy that just passed us? He must be 55 or 60 and he just strolled by like he was walking down a city street. It's killin' me."

"Let's come back here in one year," Gretchen said.

Gretchen of Wisconsin

"We can train for it and we'll hike up to the lake. Maybe even go on to the top of ..." she looked around, picking out a peak. "That one. Do you know its name?"

He didn't. But he noticed that the mountain she had selected was not the highest around. It was maybe third highest. He estimated it to be a little over 13,000 feet because he knew the middle one was Kit Carson, a "fourteener," clearly the tallest in this group. He doubted they would be able to make that ascent a year from now, but her suggestion meant something else. She wanted to come back here with *him*. When was the last time a girl had made a similar proposal to him? Never?

He turned to look into her eyes. It was one of those movie moments when there will either be a kiss or an awkward, embarrassing change of subject, a moment with *lost opportunity* written over it forever in future reminiscences. They brought their lips together in what was at first, a pretty abstinent sort of a kiss; then tongues became involved and Frank knew that if their bellies had not served as a blockade to the lower regions of their bodies, she'd notice more than his tongue and they might be tempted to rethink their recent pledges.

After dinner, Gretchen had a relapse of her headache and once again found herself hugging the toilet. They hiked again the next day, stopping to kiss or hold hands, making certain promises to each other about keeping in touch, or perhaps exchanging visits during the school year or at vacation periods. There seemed no need at this point, to discuss the voracity of their celibacy pledges. But if the time came, they were both prepared in their hearts to honor the promises they had made to the world here.

*

When Frank Jr. arrived back at school, people commented on his appearance.

"You been on a diet, JR? You look good, man."

He hadn't really noticed, but when more and more people commented, he took a critical look at himself and it was true; he was appreciably slimmer in the face, and maybe around his middle, but that wasn't all.

Frank Jr. had taken on an aura, the familiar glow that surrounds a person in love.

Back in Stevens Point, people took notice of the changes in Gretchen too. There were words of praise for her weight loss also, which like Frank, she had not even been aware of. Friends demanded to know her dieting secret. And then there was, of course— the glow.

They called each other most nights on their free nights and weekends plans.

"My friends all say I've lost a bunch of weight," Frank said.

"Me too! I didn't even know it. How is that possible in just a week?"

"It must be all those walks we took," Frank said. "Also, I didn't eat a lot. And I didn't really like the food that much. Still ..."

"I know. Same here. You know what it could be though," Gretchen said. "It could be that we were so fat, that we burned off lots of excess quickly. Fat's just nature's way of storing up for when it is called upon. Once the fat is gone, you have to start burning muscle. I don't expect that will ever happen to me. But anyway, from here on in, it will get much harder."

"What will get harder?"

"To keep it off," she said. "To keep losing more."

"You're going to try to lose more?" he asked.

"Yeah, I want to be thin. Just think what that would feel like. You know, JR, I didn't mean that you were that fat, but you'd probably feel better if you kept on losing."

"I feel fine. But if you're going to do it, I will too, up to a point."

Gretchen of Wisconsin

"Ok," she said, "I'll come down at Thanksgiving. Lets see who's lost the biggest percentage of total weight."

"Does that mean you're going to tell me what you weigh now?"

"No, silly. Just keep your own records and don't lie," she said. "I'm going to keep up my walking and cut down on snacks and second helpings."

"You're on," he said. He paused. "You know, Gretchen, you don't have to be thin for me. I like you the way you are."

She didn't answer. She was looking at herself in the mirror, imagining the possibilities.

"Change of subject," Frank said.

"OK."

"How's your artwork going?"

"Oh fine, I guess. How's your music?"

But it was clear that these had become secondary issues.

Gretchen plucked the photo from her dresser. How old had she been in this picture? It must have been taken before her father left her. Was it Gretchen he left, or was it her mother? *He* must have taken the picture. The tips of his boots showed at the very bottom of the snapshot. Her mother's hair, still dark and luxurious, spread out over the snow-covered earth. The picture had been taken from above. The two of them ... laughing, lying next to each other in the snow, arms and legs splayed like Leonardo da Vinci's drawing of the human proportions.

She was so flat. That was before she had sought out food for its medicinal effects.

She replaced the picture next to her newly framed photo of Frank Jr. and fell backward onto the bed which, received her bulk with a groan of protest. Gretchen reviewed her week in Colorado, trying to come up with just what it was that had caused her weight loss. Then she hit on it.

The vomiting.

Frank Jr. began with walks. He walked three miles a day, but gradually he found that walking took up too much of his time, so he began to run for short segments of his course, just to get it over with sooner. Then one day he realized that he could keep running beyond the point of discomfort. After all, the discomfort would end when he got to the finish line. In only a month, he found that he could run the entire course without stopping. This alone was such a feeling of accomplishment that he almost didn't notice, as October rolled around, that he had shed thirty pounds. He added a new vow to his vow of celibacy.

"From this time forward, I will run at least two miles a day until the day I die," he promised his reflection.

Most days he was able to stick to his guns. When some unforeseen event caused him to miss a day, he suffered greatly from guilt. The pounds fell away. Frank didn't change his dietary habits all that much, except to avoid between-meal snacks and his switch from regular to diet soda, which was a little hard at first, but after a while you got used to the unnatural taste of its bitter chemistry.

He felt good about himself for the first time in his life. His new size 36 jeans were still a bit snug, but the image he saw in the mirror was that of *a regular guy*. Nevertheless, he put all his old size 45's in a drawer—just in case.

Frank Jr. went downtown with his friends on Thursdays. Frank always drank Cokes while his buddies got smashed. He was the designated driver. But now he didn't want the calories in Coke, so he stuck to his diet soda or bottled water. The next thing he noticed was that girls were paying attention. Inside, he felt like the same nerd he had always been, but apparently that didn't show though his new, fit exterior. They seemed to see only the

Gretchen of Wisconsin

regular guy, and a not too bad-looking one at that. In fact, it was pretty clear that one blonde in particular—Stephanie was her name—an English major from Vandy, was definitely coming on to him. Frank played along, but he had made another vow to himself; he would be true to his Dairyland sweetheart.

On the phone to Gretchen, he described his days, which consisted mostly of study, his individual piano instruction with Dr. Evers, and his daily run.

"Dr. Evers thinks I should enter this competition in Atlanta. If I place third or better, he's going to prepare me for the *Van Clyburn* in Dallas."

"That's great," Gretchen said. "How's your weight coming?"

It was pretty clear she wasn't all that interested in his future career posturing.

"What do you think the percentage is?" she asked.

"I don't know. I'll just surprise you. We'll see each other in a week and a half. I will say this though; regardless of the weight, I've never felt better. Running has changed my life. Are you still walking? You could probably try jogging some. It's so great."

"I walked at first but, I don't know, I guess I'm not driven like you. I'm just sticking with my diet."

"How's your painting coming?" Frank asked. "You were going to enter that show in Milwaukee."

"Oh, I don't know. The deadline passed and I didn't really have anything. But my roommate Sarah—she got one piece in."

In her dorm room, Gretchen lay awake. She hadn't had the energy to actually go to class for two weeks now. She had the room to herself. Sarah, who only came in occasionally to pick up something, spent most nights at her boyfriend's apartment. It was Gretchen's job to cover for her when her parents called.

"Oh sorry, Mrs. Jansen, you just missed her. I think

she went to the studio. I'll have her call you." Then she would leave a message at Jason's apartment for Sarah to call her mom.

Messages were piling up on Gretchen's email from the Office of Student Retention. The subject line was *at-risk student*. But after the first one, she never opened them again. Lying on her back, she felt her abdomen, reveling in its new flatness. There was still a slight swell just above her pubic area but she felt certain that would soon be gone too. She ran her hands up higher to where they encountered two protruding points of resistance. It was a delightful feeling—the edges of her ribcage.

She had always known that she *had* ribs somewhere under all that flesh, but now here they were. She moved her hands up higher, allowing the tips of her fingers to work over each rib, playing them like the keys of JR's piano. She moved one hand up to caress the nipple of her new, smaller breast. She allowed the other to work its way back down over the slight swell and on down between her now thin thighs. She tried to imagine JR, probing the new Gretchen, but the only face she could come up with was Brian, a guy she had met at a bar in downtown Stevens Point. Brian was good looking, on the tennis team, a guy who, before her new improved self, wouldn't have given her the time of day. But he had been all over her.

So much for that pledge.

There had been a few others since Brian. She wasn't really interested in any of them, not in the same way she was interested in JR, but he was in Nashville and they were here in Wisconsin. She got up and walked to the desk, naked. She admired the silhouette of her body—her new toy—in the mirror over her dresser. She opened the drawer and helped herself from her stock of Snickers bars.

Then she went into the bathroom and stuck a finger down her throat.

Gretchen of Wisconsin

Frank Jr. met her at the Nashville airport. At first they both looked past each other. At last, a spark of recognition showed when their eyes locked. They kissed, a friendly sort of kiss, then—they held each other at arms length to get a better look. It was clear that they would have to reestablish their familiarity, as each had shed an entire person. The voices were the same they recognized from their telephone conversations but the experience was somewhat like seeing a radio personality for the first time.

Frank took her to his school, showed her the practice room where he prepared for his recital in Atlanta, played Beethoven's *Moonlight Sonata* for her, took her to Vanderbilt's football game where they endured the painful first half of what Frank's friend Chris, called Tennessee's annual Commodore ass-kicking, then took her out to dinner. At the restaurant, she picked at her entrée, but ate all of her Double Chocolate Fudge Devil's Temptation before excusing herself. She was in the bathroom for what Frank thought was an extraordinary length of time. When she returned, looking somewhat pale, he had long since paid the bill.

"You OK?" he asked. "You don't look so good."

"I'm fine. Just a little tired from the trip I think. It's been a long day. Look, I know you wanted to show me around some more, but could we just go back to your apartment? I'm really exhausted."

"Sure."

Frank was a bit nervous about what would come next. His roommate was gone for the weekend. But there was the pledge. This was going to be a little awkward and it was undeniable; he ached for her. But a promise is a promise, and Frank was a man of conviction.

They listened to music and watched some TV until it was time for bed. Frank had cleaned the apartment to the point that it looked better than most men's apartments ever do. He had even scrubbed the toilet bowl. His bed was made up with clean sheets and pillowcases. It would be hers while he slept on the couch. When Gretchen emerged from the bathroom in a revealing, pink he-didn't-know-what-to-call-it, he had to avert his eyes.

"Well," he said, "if there's anything you need, I …"

Gretchen came over and snuggled up to him, taking his hand and guiding it up under the delicate garment to her breast while deep kissing him. Frank pulled back.

"We made our pledges, remember?"

"Fuck those pledges."

Frank was somewhat taken aback by her unexpected dirty mouth.

"We were fat. It's easy to swear off sex when you're fat. We're thin now. Are you sure you want to miss out on this?" She pushed his hand lower.

"But since I made the pledge, I … I'm not … you know … prepared. I don't have anything for … protection."

Gretchen stepped away and reached into her purse, unfurling an accordion of condoms. She tore one off and handed it to him. Frank Jr. considered for a moment, the ramifications of a girl who carried, what for him would have been a lifetime supply of condoms in her purse, but the situation being what it was, he abandoned his principles and his questions and let nature take its course.

*

"Well," Gretchen said, lying on her back with her hands folded behind her head, "since you lost all that weight, I can see it's made you very *fast*."

"I'm sorry," he said, "you know, that was my first time."

"You'll get better at it. You know what?"

"Tell me," he said.

If we had gone say, seven minutes—in that position—we would have burned twenty calories."

He propped himself up on one elbow to look at her.

"I'd say that was good for about ten for you and six for me. Next time we'll do it from the rear. That's supposed to burn forty. I don't run like you, so I need the exercise. Now get yourself ready, Bucko. Let's see if you can stay in the saddle a little longer."

"Your scientific approach is going to corrupt me," he said.

She slapped his buttocks and reached across him to the bedside table, ripping off another packet. During the remainder of the weekend they got enough exercise that Frank Jr. didn't feel guilty about neglecting his run, although as Gretchen pointed out, twenty minutes of jogging burns 189 calories.

*

"When will I see you again?" Frank asked her at the airport check-in.

She was softer now, not as oddly tough and demanding as she had seemed throughout the weekend. He had almost gotten to the point where he didn't *like* her. But now she seemed sweet again and his love began once more to overtake his lust.

"I have to go home for Christmas with my parents," she said.

"Me too, but what about the week after?"

"I can't get away. What if we went back to Colorado over Spring Break? It must be pretty there in the snow. We could go snow shoeing."

"I don't know if I'd get very far," he said. "I tried it once and I kept crossing them over each other and tripping."

"You'll get used to it. We do it all the time in Wisconsin. Besides, you're a quick study with me showing you the ropes." She winked.

They made arrangements to fly into Colorado Springs in March. They would rent a car and drive to Sled

Lake. The camp would be closed of course, but there was a motel, and besides, she wanted to show off to Brandy, one of the skinny girls from camp who worked at the restaurant in town.

Back at school, Gretchen tried to get back into an academic groove. She started going to classes again, although she had to beg and cajole, to get her instructors to allow her back. She explained how she had come down with mono, and she could bring doctors excuses if they insisted. But she found that a gentle touch to the arm, an accidental grazing of breast on sleeve, the tossing of hair and pouting of lips, were all the excuse necessary. She had observed these successful maneuvers performed by thin girls in the past, from behind her chunky camouflage. Unfortunately, it didn't work out in every case. One of her professors was a woman.

The winter passed in phone calls and emails. When they met at the Springs airport, Frank was alarmed when he saw her. She had shriveled from slender to downright emaciated. Her jawbones protruded at a squarish angle from her tiny neck. Her face, though still pretty, had a hollowness about it that allowed an observer to understand precisely, the relationship of the human form to the skull beneath it.

"Gretchen! You …you're *too* thin," he said as he drew her to him for a kiss.

"Oh, you sound like my mom. She keeps saying, 'too thin, too skinny.' I feel kind of chubby actually. *You* look thinner," she said. "You look great."

Frank had increased the distance of his daily run. He ate like a horse now but his weight had stabilized at a healthy 195 or so, redistributed mostly as muscle.

She could see her own distorted reflection in the window as they walked toward the baggage claim. She was always on the lookout for it. She watched its translucent, concentration camp facsimile pass in front of the hulking shoulder of Pikes Peak on the other side of the glass.

They drove to Sled Lake in their rented Hyundai Accent, or as Frank called it, Hyundai Accident. The little car struggled to carry Frank Jr., their luggage, and his weightless girlfriend up the mountain. They went straight to the Early Bird Restaurant where Brandy worked. Frank was starving. Brandy didn't recognize either of them until they explained who they were. Her shock, when the moment of recognition finally came, registered on her face. She looked at Frank with what could be described as admiration and at Gretchen with what could only be described as—a sense of horror.

Frank ordered a steak and Gretchen took about three bites of a salad. When she left the table to disappear for her usual inordinate amount of time in the bathroom, Brandy came over.

"What's wrong with her? It's not something serious, I hope."

Frank didn't have an answer. He just looked at her, trying to think of something. His face must have registered a concern that, to Brandy, was some kind of explanation.

Brandy clamped her hand over her mouth and looked at him through expressive big eyes. "It's cancer, isn't it?" she said, slowly removing her hand from her face.

But before he could dissuade Brandy of that notion, Gretchen came back from the bathroom looking pale as usual, and even lighter in weight—if that was possible.

In the Sled Lake Inn, they made love. It was easy for Frank now. His principles and his inhibitions had long since been discarded. Her body felt so much different than it had back in Nashville. He had never felt anything like it. She seemed only marginally human. He imagined making love to one of those creatures that you always saw descending the ramp of a flying saucer. Her head even seemed disproportionately large, the same as the aliens.

He felt embarrassed about his own muscular form. He ran his hands over his torso, probing for ribs. He went to sleep, intending to ask for her secrets in the morning.

Gretchen lay awake for some time listening to Frank's slow, steady breathing. The feeling in her shrunken stomach produced the kind of high—she thought—that junkies must get from crack or heroine. It was the delicious pang of hunger. Hunger was her friend. Having allowed basically nothing, to remain in her stomach longer than a minute or two for the past three days, she felt so happy—and clean. The laxatives had purified the remainder of her digestive tract. She was also certain that she had now reached what she had thought previously to be an unattainable goal. The fat was gone. She was beginning to burn off the unwanted weight of muscle.

At last she fell asleep but woke again in an hour, still high on malnutrition, altitude and the instructions she had received just now in a vision—from Jesus himself.

Frank awoke to cold. Gretchen was not in the bed beside him. It was still dark. He looked at the bedside clock. Four-twenty-six. The cold entered through the door that stood open directly onto the single story motel's parking lot. He could see the moon's reflection off the Hyundai's windshield.

"Gretchen? Gretchen?"

He pulled his jeans on and slipped, sockless, into his loafers. He shrugged into his leather jacket without putting on a shirt and went out into the sub-zero early morning, calling quietly, "Gretchen! Gretchen!"

It was hours before he found her.

He had gone back to the room to put on warmer clothing. When the sky lightened he rang the bell at the front desk. A sleepy looking desk clerk emerged from behind a closed door.

"We don't put the coffee out 'til six thirty," the guy said, when he saw Frank Jr. absently staring in the direction of the coffee maker.

"Listen," Frank said, "I'm sorry to bother you so early but my ... my girlfriend ...has disappeared."

The desk clerk merely looked at him. Frank could see in the guy's face, that it wasn't really his problem.

"I mean," he said, "she's just gone. Walked out of the room in the middle of the night and ... her clothes are still there. The car is still there."

He pointed toward the little Hyundai, then made a sweeping gesture, taking in the entire valley.

"She's out there somewhere. You gotta help, or at least call the police. OK?"

But by the time the local deputy arrived, Frank had found her. No wonder he had not seen her until the sun was up full. She was behind the motel, lying below the level of the snow, in an area that she had obviously scraped out for herself. Her paper-thin profile was only visible from above. There would be questions. He knew enough not to move her. But he was sure that the scene would be self-explanatory. He would not fall under suspicion when they saw her. He felt weak and guilty—thinking of himself at a time like this, but he knew it would be best for him to leave her as she was—a naked skeletal form, eyes open to the sky, in that familiar position he had himself, once assumed—the first time his parents had taken him north—the first time he saw snow—the first time he had made a snow angel.

Low-Rider

Edna hears the car pull into her driveway.
 She looks up from her paper to the calendar. Yes, it's Thursday. That would be that nice boy from the pharmacy with her prescriptions. What was his name again? Donnie or ... or ... Joey? Joey, she thinks. Yes, she's

almost sure it's Joey. But this car sounds different, louder. She pushes aside the sheer curtains of the window next to her dinette set. This car *looks* different too. Seems like Donnie or Joey's car didn't have those black windows.

And the motor or the muffler—they're certainly very loud, very rumbley. There's another noise, a loud thumping noise coming from inside the car, a cacophony so powerful that it rattles the dishes in her cabinet with each *whump-whump*. She covers her ears with her hands but that doesn't stop the heavy noise from penetrating into her chest. She can feel the *whump* in her bones, as though some living thing has moved in and taken over the workload of her own weak heart.

There. They've turned it off.

Thank heavens. My, oh my. What a terrible racket. She'll have to remember to call Mr. Perkins and remind him not to send this *thumper* car next time. And just look at all those colors. She wonders why they make cars nowadays that have different colored hoods and doors like that. She watches the car in her driveway, waiting for Joey to get out and bring in her prescriptions. She has her money ready—and his cookies. He's a nice boy. He likes her chocolate chip cookies. He doesn't like milk though. Likes Coca Cola. Now that's funny. Milk is so good with cookies. Who'd want ruin it with Co …

Oh good. Somebody' getting out of the passenger side. A tall, skinny blonde girl. Edna hasn't seen a girl come before. Maybe Joey has a sister. She shades her eyes against the bright sun with one hand. She leans into the car to tell the driver something but then she straightens up again and just keeps staring at the house.

Maybe they think this is the wrong address. It would be nice if she could see into the car but—those windows. How do they see to drive? Well, she'll just have to go out and tell them that they've got the address right. She pushes herself away from the table, but as she does, she sees the driver's door open. A praying mantis of a boy, unfolds himself into the sunlight. She feels a pang of recognition and memory that sends a shiver through her, causing her fingers to tingle.

Clarence?

But it can't be Clarence. Besides, Clarence was old and he didn't have stringy blonde hair like this boy, and—no tattoos.

She remembers now, that awful day that she tries so hard not to think about—Clarence standing out in the backyard while she washed dishes. He had gone out there for something—to smoke maybe, or feed the dog. Which dog was that? Was that Buddy, or Skipper? She remembers some movement that caught her eye. She turned away from the sink and watched him fall right over. It looked like that slow motion they do on television sometimes. She doesn't like thinking about that. Still, it happens from time to time but she doesn't cry about it any more. What's done is done.

Her front door has windows on each side of it. In each window there's a face pressed up, hands cupped around it looking in. Joey always rings the bell. That darned doorbell must be broken again. She'll have to call Sally. Sally's husband, Jim is so handy. He can probably fix it for her. Costs an arm and a leg if you have to call the electricians.

She makes her way slowly to the door. Just as she reaches for the door handle, she sees that the latch is jiggling. *Well hold your horses. I'm a-comin'.* She opens the door and sees that the boy looks kind of surprised. He's fooling with some little piece of wire or something.

"Hello," Edna says.

"Uh ... hi," the boy says.

"I guess that doorbell's stopped working," she says.

"Um."

"Were you tryin' to fix it with that wire?"

The boy doesn't say anything.

"That's right," the girl says.

"Now, you're not Joey, I know that. Joey's not nearly as tall as you." She surveys his length. "My goodness! You must be Donnie."

The boy still doesn't say anything but the blonde girl answers for him.

"Yeah. He's Donnie."

The girl looks at Donnie and smiles at him with her eyes.

"Right," Donnie says.

"And what's your name, Hon?" Edna asks.

"Me? I'm ... I'm Amber."

Donnie looks at Amber like it's the first time he's ever heard her name.

"So, did you bring my drugs?"

Donnie and Amber swap glances again.

"That's right," Amber says.

"Well, why don't you come on in and have some cookies first? Now, I know that Joey always likes Coke with his cookies. Is that what you want too, or would you like milk?"

"You got *coke*?" Donnie says. His eyes get big.

Enda notices that Amber pokes Donnie in the side with her elbow because Donnie says "Ow," and frowns at her.

"Milk would be fine," Amber says.

While Amber sits at the table with her milk and cookies, *that* Donnie walks around the house picking up things and examining them, dropping crumbs everywhere he goes. She's going to have to go around with the vacuum when they're gone. They stay for quite a while. They ask lots of questions, the kind of questions you'd think would have been answered by the people at the drugstore. What kind of drugs did she order? Which ones does she have on hand now? Where does she keep them? She wishes they'd just go get them out of the car now and leave her be. She has a few things to do and it's almost noon now. She doesn't want to be rude, but she hates to miss the noon news and weather.

The phone rings. Edna starts to get up but Amber jumps up and says, "No, you sit. Have another cookie. I'll get it."

She hears a sound from the other room where the phone is, a sort of snapping noise, then she hears Amber talking, "No. Sorry but we've had to change our policy. We get so many of these calls that we can no longer accept them. Goodbye."

"Was that my friend Helen?" Edna asks, when Amber returns. "She was supposed to call about taking me out to Wal-Mart."

"No, it was some guy from … from the … Vietnam Veterans. I told him that you get too many of these kind of calls and they shouldn't expect you to give them anything 'cause you don't have that much yourself."

"Oh dear. I don't know. I feel bad about that. Maybe I should call him back."

"No! He said that he understood and that they meant to take your name off the list anyway and that they're sorry and they won't bother you any more."

"He said all that? It didn't seem like you were even on the phone that long, dear. And the Vietnam veterans … they had such a hard time, you know. Our boy Dennis was over there. He said you couldn't tell one gook from another so he shot at all of them. I think he was terribly upset by it all. Now where did that Donnie get to?"

Edna looks around for the skinny pharmacy delivery boy.

Donnie rounds a corner, smiling. He's holding up a little brown medicine bottle. "Looks like you're getting kind of low on this one. We'll take it back and get it refilled for you."

"Which one is that?" Edna asks, squinting at the little container. "No. That's my pain medicine. I just had that filled. There should be plenty of that."

"Nope," Donnie says. "Practically empty." He pockets it. "Listen, Lady,"

"Oh, please, call me Edna."

Edna sees Amber narrow her eyes at Donnie.

"Listen, Edna, I need to make a phone call. That be OK?"

"There could be a problem with the phone," Amber says, raising her brow.

"Oh no," Edna says. "The phone's not working?"

Amber gets up to discuss something with Donnie that Edna can't hear. They go out of the room together for a minute. When they come back Amber says, "Your friend, the one that was going to take you to Wal-mart?"

"You mean Helen?"

"Right, Helen. Well, they told us at the drugstore that we were supposed to take you 'cause Helen's sick."

"They knew that Helen was supposed to take me to Wal-Mart?"

Edna looks puzzled. "I hope it's nothing serious," she says.

"No, no, just a little cough. She'll be right as rain in a couple of days." Then she added, "They said."

Just then, there's a knock at the door.

"Um, I'll get it," Donnie says. "You just relax."

Gosh, Edna thinks, they're so thoughtful.

Edna hears some mumbling at the door. She can make out a few words from Donnie—none from the other person.

"No, sorry. She can't come to the door right now."

Pause.

"That's fine. You can leave it with me. I'll give it to her."

Pause.

"Yeah."

Pause.

"No, no. It's not serious. She'll be OK in a couple days. Yeah, OK. What's she owe ya?"

Pause.

"Ok. Hang on a sec."

Donnie comes back into the kitchen.

"Guy needs thirty bucks. Delivery."

"Oh my!" Edna says. "My purse is over there in the basket next to the Refrigerator."

Donnie brings it to her. She counts out twenty-eight dollars and some change.

"That's close enough," Donnie says.

He goes back and gives the guy fifteen.

Edna looks out the window to see the car pull out of the drive. She recognizes it. It's the usual car from the drugstore, the one with the mortar and pestle on the door. Suddenly, Edna is uncomfortable with Donnie and Amber.

"I thought *you* were from the drug store," she says.

"It's all right," Donnie says. "I told them we were short, so they sent the other guy out with the rest of your order."

Edna considers this for a moment.

"But, I thought the phone ..."

Donnie looks over the bottles. Hands them to her.

It must be OK. They seem to know best. The girl is nice. She'd be pretty even, if her hair were just a ...

"Hey, Chri- ... Amber ... hadn't you better be getting along to that Wal-Mart gig?"

Amber helps Edna to her feet and together they shuffle toward the door.

"Listen, Amber, when you get to Wal-Mart give Terry a call."

Amber gives him a puzzled look.

"You know, Terry? With the truck." He winks.

Low Rider

"You're not coming along?" Edna says. "I don't know …"

"No," Donnie says. "You two go on now. You have a good time. I'm going to be working on some stuff here—fixing a few things. You know Terry?" he says to Edna. "The guy with the truck? Well he's a telephone repair dude. We'll get that phone fixed up. In fact, I already been workin' on a few things while you and Chri-…Amber here, was talkin' out in the kitchen."

Amber shoots another puzzled expression his way. "Look at this."

He escorts the two women to the front porch where he presses the button of the doorbell. The first eight tones of Beethoven's hand of fate, (Clarence's little joke,) greet the group, clearly indicating that Donnie's repair skills have been put to good use since his arrival.

"You fixed the doorbell!" Edna says with delight. "Well, I swear. You're just about as handy as Sally's husband, Jim."

Amber helps Edna into the car, holding onto her arm while she lowers herself in. Amber has to brush some crumbs off the seat and toss a few cans into the back where they clank against other cans before nestling into some paper trash. When Amber turns the key in the ignition, a healthy dose of *whump-whumping* blasts out from the two carpet-covered boxes mounted in the rear window, causing Edna to cover her ears. Amber reaches over and turns the sound system off. "Sorry," she says. "Donnie likes his music loud."

"Is that what that was?" Edna asks.

Edna examines the dark windows from inside now. She's surprised that she can even see out.

"What kind of car *is* this?"

"A Pontiac, I think. It's a low-rider."

Edna can't remember ever hearing about a Pontiac Low Rider. Clarence's friend, Otto Stromberg used to have a Pontiac Bonneville.

At Wal-Mart, Edna allows Amber to secure for her, one of those little motorized carts. She doesn't really need it. She can walk, slowly and with only a minimum of pain, but with Amber showing her how to operate the electric controls, it's really kind of fun. They cruise through old-lady underwear, old-lady shoes and old-lady handbags. Amber lobs the items Edna picks out, into the basket.

"You remind me of my daughter," Edna says.

It's been years since she went shopping with her daughter. She wants to buy something for Amber.

"Where is she now?" Amber asks.

"Chicago."

"What's her name?"

"Sarah," Edna says. "She married an architect. I don't get to see her very much. Maybe once a year." Edna cups her hand to her mouth and signals Amber to come closer. "I don't think he likes me," she whispers. "He comes from money—Boston. Us Hoosiers aren't good enough for 'im."

On their way through womens' underwear, Amber runs her hand over a pair of delicate mauve panties.

"Those are pretty aren't they?" Edna says. "Why don't you get yourself a few pair? My treat. You've been so sweet to me. You and Donnie."

Amber hesitates for a moment, then removes the panties from the rack and tosses them in the basket along with two more pair, one of which, is such a skimpy little item that causes Edna to purse her lips into a silent whistle. Amber smiles a naughty-girl smile. Edna giggles, covering her mouth so that the laughter only escapes from her gray eyes. They continue on toward the checkout but Edna suggests that they make a detour into the toiletries where she buys Amber bubble bath, lotions, make-up, hair care products and a general sampling of the very best that Wal-Mart has to offer. Edna almost wishes that Amber were a

Low Rider 67

bit younger, remembering the thrill she always got from back-to-school shopping for Dennis and Sarah.

"Now, it wouldn't be nice," Edna says patting Amber on the arm, "for us girls to have all this fun shopping and come home without a thing for poor Donnie. Let's run back to the hardware and get him a little tool set or something. Men always love tools."

"You don't have to do that. He …"

Edna cuts her off.

"Now, Child, I want to do this. Come on."

Edna's an expert cart driver by now. She's glad the hardware is on the other side of the store from the toiletries so she can maneuver the vehicle a bit longer, leaning ever so slightly into each turn.

As they peruse the electric tools, Edna tells Amber about when Clarence used to take her shopping. "He was so bored. He used to just sit in a chair while I tried on dresses and such at Sears Roebuck. I'd model things for him and he'd always say, 'that looks nice.' Then I'd catch him looking at his watch. You know how they do." Clara nudges Amber and gives her a knowing frown. "But as long as he left with a pair of pliers or a screwdriver, he was happy enough. Sometimes we'd go out for a bite to eat afterwards. He used to love to go to Mac's Barbeque but they closed that down." Edna gets a dreamy expression.

They leave the store with their many purchases, which include an air-wrench for Donnie. Edna doesn't want to go home. She suggests they eat at Long John Silver's then make a quick run through the Mall. Now that she knows about the electric carts, she has Amber search for one at the Mall as well. This one is a little different and she has to learn the controls all over again, but gets the hang of it pretty quickly. They pass a beauty salon right there in the Mall where everybody walking by can see you get your hair cut, or died or washed. Edna feels that this lack of privacy is disquieting but suggests that they take advantage of the convenience. It's been ages since Edna had her hair tended to by a professional, so she gets a wash and set and she pays for a new cut for Amber.

At last they leave the mall. It's almost dark now. They both feel pretty and happy. Amber squeezes Edna's arm. Amber's new cut is perky. Edna thinks she looks like that girl from *You've Got Mail*. Edna is not excited about the prospect of dropping back into the seat of the loud, low car with the dark windows, but she knows that this is the only way home.

"Thank you, dear," Edna says, "I just had the nicest day."

"Me too," says Amber, without looking at her, her voice breaking ever so slightly. Edna gives her arm a little squeeze. Amber keeps her eyes straight ahead but Edna sees one small tear leak from the corner of Amber's eye. Amber quickly swats at it, as though some insect has landed there. She sniffles softly and drives on.

They round the corner onto Edna's street. The house is dark. Donnie and his friend with the truck must have finished up and left.

"Won't you come in for a cup of tea?" Edna says.

"No thanks," Amber says, "I need to get going."

Amber seems suddenly distant. She merely reaches across Edna to open the door for her. She doesn't help her get out of the car. It's difficult to get yourself up from this low seat. It take three or four strong efforts to stand, get all her bags and start up the walk.

"Thanks again," Edna says, leaning down to look in at Amber, who keeps her eyes glued to some invisible spot beyond the windshield. "I just had a lovely day."

Without turning toward her, Amber gives a little wave and begins to pull away. Edna watches for a moment as the car slowly rumbles toward the end of the block. She opens her door and puts the packages down on the floor before she turns on the light. Something hard inside one of her shopping bags, when it makes contact with the floor, echoes though her house. A hollow, empty sound surrounds her in the dark. She flips on the light. Is this her house? Could Amber have dropped her off at some newly constructed house? She steps back outside the door to check the house number. Amber's car has turned at the end of the street. Surely she has realized her mistake and is coming back to pick her up and take her to the proper street, but she drives on by. Edna presses the doorbell. The opening of Beethoven's Fifth blends with the fading rumble of the multi-colored low-rider as it disappears around the corner.

Spiderhole

3:35 AM: I need to pee.
There's probably no one else in the building. Probably nothing to worry about, but it really makes me nervous. I could slip my clothes on and if someone sees me, I'd just pretend I'm working late.

Spiderhole

"Oh hey, how ya doin? Workin' late too I see. Heh heh."

I'd stretch my arms.

"I'm a little stiff from having my eyes glued to the computer all night," I might say.

But my hair's a dead giveaway. As my son would say, I got a bad case of bedhead.

But it's too much trouble to get dressed so I stand quietly just inside my door, listening. There are sounds out there in the hallway, but I think it's just the clock. Every now and then I hear a click. Slowly—quietly, I unlock the deadbolt and turn the knob. Nothing.

In my socks and underwear, I pad down the deserted hall to the bathroom. It's weird. In about five hours I'll be walking down these same halls, like the respectable scholar my students assume me to be. I'll look at my notes and begin my lecture, just like all their other professors. At the end of the day, if they think about me at all—and why should they—they'll assume that I go home to my wife and kids or some other normal life, girlfriend—dog maybe.

I don't flush. Don't want to make any noise. I shuffle quickly back to my office and lock the door. I try to get back to sleep on my folding cot.

I do have a wife and kids actually—and a dog—and a girlfriend. All of them are asleep right now, in homes or apartments or doghouses. I won't have the wife much longer. The divorce will be final soon.

The girlfriend was probably a mistake, but when you've been with a woman so long, it's hard to suddenly be without one. She's young—my girlfriend. One of my students, of course—Syndi.

How awful—her name I mean. How could her parents have named her Syndi? What's wrong with Cynthia or Cindy? Syndi sounds like some kind of porn star. Like Sin. She's a sinner and her name is some sort of testament to that fact. Now that I think about it, she could be a fairly good one actually. Porn star I mean.

I didn't want to be like every other male prof I know. Always ogling the female students. I'm embarrassed about it now. It's so predictable.

What's that? It's not on this floor. The elevator maybe. I sit up on my cot to get a better listening angle. Shit. It's nothing. Get some sleep.

The next time I look, it's 5:30. My bladder is full again but I'm not going out there half naked this time. Might as well get dressed and get out of here before Luke gets in at 6:00. My first class isn't until 10:30. I don't have anywhere to go, really. I guess I could go to breakfast.

I step out of my door and almost collide with Luke.

"How you doin,' Dave?"

Luke works first shift. He calls all of us by our first names. Students are very uncomfortable with the first name basis, sometimes even when you have been intimate with them. But it finally it sinks in that you're not just Dr. Roberts. You're a real person with a first name, irritating habits and frustrating foibles. Hair grows out of your ears and nostrils. You emit foul gasses during the night.

"You're workin' early," Luke points out.

"Yup," I say. "I Like to take advantage of the quiet. I can think better." I pat my briefcase as proof that I've already been hard at it.

At Denny's, I'm one of the first customers. I order the Original Scram Slam, which I eat while reading the paper. After breakfast I head back to campus to hang out in the library until a half hour before class. When I return to my office there are messages on my machine. Two are from Jenny. She hopes I'm OK, but I think that's just a courtesy, as she goes on to remind me that this is my weekend with the kids. She's going out of town. She doesn't say where and I find that I am unreasonably jealous. I suspect she's going somewhere with her neurologist. Are those proper professional ethics? He ought to be fired.

Why should I care? After all, I dumped her. Traded her in on a newer model.

I should be fired.

What will they do together? I know what she likes. I see her on her knees, moaning and gripping the pillow her face is pushed into. "Yes, yes—Oh god—give it to me," She says.

The kids.

"When are you coming home, Daddy?"

I try to be a good dad. They want to know what happened.

"Things happen sometimes with adults," I explain. "It doesn't have anything to do with you guys. It's not your fault. Mom and Dad just can't be together any more."

"Mommy cries a lot," Lucy says.

Chad says little. He pouts. He's angry with me.

I'll take them to the cabin on the lake. That's where I tell everyone I live. It's OK to be there on weekends but it's too far to drive in every day. After the money I give Jenny, there's just not enough left to get an apartment.

The other message is from Syndi.

"I need to talk to you. Please come over tonight. I'm making pasta. We can rent a movie. OK? Call me."

I can't do this any more. I just want my life back. Alone.

I see myself living in the mountains. Colorado or Wyoming. I'll be a mountain man like Jeremiah Johnson. I'll hunt griz. Truth is, there are only two things that scare the shit out of me . . getting fat . . . and griz.

Maybe Colorado. I think they only have black bears there. I'll hunt black bear.

I've been trying to let Syndi down easily. I appreciate everything she's done for me, but I want out now. After work I go over to her apartment. She's reading on the couch when I come in. I feel sorry for her because she's reading. I have done this to her. I forced her out. I've caused her to sit alone, reading, in a dingy apartment. But I couldn't stand being in the cabin with her another day.

You said you were going to get your own place, I reminded her day after day until she finally did. I'll spend time at your apartment now and then, I said. Nothing would change, I said. I just can't have you living here when the kids come, I said.

But when she packed her two small boxes of belongings, I felt a weight lifted from my shoulders. I felt free.

"Look," I explain to her now, after the fine dinner she prepares. "You should find someone your own age. Look at this body." I grab two handfuls of middle-aged gut. "When you're thirty-five, I'll be . . ." I try to calculate.

"Forty-nine," she says helpfully. "I don't care. I love you. Age isn't important. I want to take care of you. You need me."

"You should be going out with Biff and Scooter and Billy."

She doesn't think this is funny. She picks up the dishes and takes them to the kitchen. I don't offer to help. I'm helpless. I sit in front of the crappy 13 inch TV I brought from home. It's hers now. I gave it to her along with an old car.

Payoffs.

I paid Jenny off with a whole house, a Toyota, two-car garage, dog—money. Syndi can have anything else she wants. I'll start over with nothing.

At home I would be doing the dishes. That's my job. My part of the bargain. But I'm paralyzed here. I get up and put my Shania Twain cd into her shitty little boom box, just for the sadness of it. Syndi walks through and leans down to brush her lips across my forehead.

She hates Shania Twain. I know this already. She says Shania Twain blows. If she had been around when my musical tastes developed she would have shown me the way. She would have enlightened me.

She won't let me leave tonight. Reluctantly, I agree to stay over but in my head, I long for my office. I picture the glow from the computer screen washing over my little folding cot. The appeal is as magnetic as the image of my Colorado mountain retreat. But she's worn me down. We sit at her 1950's dinette set and she wears me down some more. She refuses to give up on me—refuses to be dumped.

I'm numbed by all the talk. Her fervent declarations of love make me sleepy. That always happens. The more serious the discussion, the more my eyes burn. I struggle to keep them open while she holds my hands and exhorts me to love her back.

"You always do this. You can't be that sleepy. We have to talk this through."

"Could we talk in bed?" I say.

In bed we hash through it all again. Eventually she fondles and squeezes until she coaxes a performance out of me that she has earned through her commitment to me, and her cooking. Thank God, she finally agrees that *I* have earned the right to sleep.

I awaken to an astounding amount of noise. It's hot in her downtown apartment. Through the open windows, the morning sounds of traffic and garbage collection, the train tracks that are a mile closer than they were to our house—are brutal. She doesn't seem to mind this. She's happy. She thinks our lovemaking has repaired all my wounds—erased all my doubts. I don't want to start this all over so I kiss her in a husbandly manner and head off to work. Just another couple, starting their daily routine.

"I can't come over tonight. I need to work. I have the kids this weekend. I'll call you Sunday night."

She's perfectly happy with this arrangement. Everything is hunky dunky now. I guess she'll read all day until she sets out for her new job as a waitress at the Mexican restaurant. A great application of her art history degree.

In my office at the end of the day, I turn the answering machine off and unplug the phone. A handful of students mill about in the building. I sit in front of my computer with the door open so everyone will see that I'm a regular hard-working soul.

"See ya Monday," Martin says. Martin's the photography instructor.

"OK, Marty. Have a nice weekend."

I should feel sorry for myself. I could leave and go out to eat at Denny's but I'm perfectly content to drop a pop tart in my toaster and make another cup of instant coffee. I keep the water on day and night. I overhear Glyndon, the night man, talking to Luke as they pass by my door.

"Does that guy live here?"

I feel a rush of adrenalin. They suspect me. But of what? The state provides me with this nice private office. I do my job. What's wrong with sleeping here? Yet somehow I know it's not acceptable. My pop tart springs up just as Brandon, one of my students, sticks his head in.

"Hey," he says.

"Pop tart," I explain, looking back toward the noise.

Brandon doesn't give a shit if I have a pop tart. I know this, but for some reason I feel it necessary to identify the sound.

"I was wondering if you would mind writing me a recommendation. I'm applying to three grad schools."

We talk a bit about the schools and what they have to offer. When he leaves I lock the door. My pop tart is cold now. I notice that the crumbs around the toaster have attracted tiny German cockroaches. I see the eggs they've laid and even little baby cockroaches, perfect miniature clones of their nasty parents. I need to get some spray next time I'm at the grocery.

Showers are the toughest.

I didn't shower at Syndi's this morning and I didn't go to the gym today, so I will have to use my system. My office is equipped with a sink. I've stopped peeing in it because it was beginning to smell. But I bought a garden hose, equipped with a sort of rubber device that fits over the faucet like a condom—and a galvanized washtub like the one the Joads must have carried from Oklahoma to the promised-land. I hook the hose up to the sink and stand in the tub. It's hard, but I manage to shower without getting too much water on the floor. I wipe up the excess and pack the tub back under the cabinet.

My clean clothes are folded neatly in all the filing cabinets that I have emptied of cameras, slides, student folders, etc. My dirty gym clothes are in towel-wrapped bundles packed under the sink next to the washtub. I've noticed a really interesting phenomenon about that. After a few days, I guess the sweaty gym stuff starts to ferment, giving off gasses. The odor is strange. My advisees who come to see me about registering for next semester's classes, seem to sniff at the air. It's not a bad odor—not like smelly gym clothes at all—just odd. But here's the really strange part. The cabinet doors won't stay closed. The gas from the fermentation forces them open so that I have to stack heavy objects against the doors to rein it in.

On Saturday I pick the kids up from Jenny's. Lucy doesn't want to let go of her mommy. Chad stands sullenly next to my new, used car—a 15 year-old silver Ford Escort station wagon. He squints into the sun.

"Where are you going?" I ask Jenny.

"Away," she says, with a roll of her eyes toward—I guess—the kids. "You can't ask me that," she says in a hushed tone. "You've given up your right to know where I go and what I do."

"And *who* you're doing," I say bitterly.

We eat at Chucky Cheese's. It's awful, but I smile and pretend I'm having a good time. They're quiet on the drive up to the cabin. A cop pull's me over on the way there.

"Had anything to drink tonight sir?"

"No sir."

"I noticed you were weaving a bit."

"I was? I ..." Then I remember. It' s the damned itching. I've just about ripped the skin off my forearms. I explain this to the guy. I show him my bloody arm. I guess while I'm tearing at it the steering wheel is wobbling. He hands me my license and warns me to be careful, but he follows us for miles while I drive with excruciating slowness until our turn-off. When I see his lights disappear I rip at the remaining flesh on my arm.

When we get there, Lucy takes down her coloring books and crayons from my bookcase and starts to draw. Chad busies himself with catching and torturing various types of insect life and I start on the first of several gins and tonics, applying some to my shredded arm as medication.

Our beds are in the loft. The kids sleep in twin trundle beds that I built myself. Chad's deep breathing is loud and comforting. I watch a porn video on the black and white TV on my dresser until I am sleepy. I don't like being here alone in the woods. I'm afraid. But with these two little kids to protect me I feel oddly safe.

On Monday the whole routine starts again. Phone messages from Syndi. Me trying to avoid her. Suspicious Janitors. On Tuesday I relent to pressure from Syndi for another dinner at her apartment. But this time I'm free to go afterward. She doesn't even try to stop me.

At the building, I don't park at the most convenient

spot, directly across the street from my office window. I'm worried about surveillance so I park about two blocks away on a residential street. From my fourth floor window I can see my car through my binoculars. I unfold my cot and turn on the little TV in my office. I pop open a can of Pabst I have stashed under the sink along with my dirty gym clothes. The beer's hot but I don't care. To my amazement, considering my sad living arrangements, I laugh at the antics of Dave Letterman as he leaps from a trampoline in his Velcro suit to adhere himself to a Velcro wall.

As usual I need the bathroom at about 3:30. I pad down the hall in my underwear again. In the bathroom, I think I hear a noise. I listen carefully to sounds through the wall. On the other side of the wall to which my ear is pressed, is the "still-life storage room." It's where we keep the junk we use in drawing and painting set-ups. I climb up on the toilet and push the ceiling panel aside. When I stick my head up in there, it's clear to me what I'm hearing. *Somebody is fucking in the still-life storage.*

When I get back to my office I feel a little strange. I'm not the only one using the place as a refuge.

In the dark office I'm aware of distant flashing blue lights. Somebody pulled over I guess. I go to the window and see that the cop's lights are about two blocks away where my car is parked. Through my binoculars, I watch as another cop car pulls up, adding his contribution to the light-show. They're out of their cruisers now, beaming flashlights into my vehicle, crouching to radio in the numbers off my plate. How can my poor little Ford Escort station wagon be the cause of such concern? I watch until they drive away. I decide to move the car. It's 4:20 now and here I am again out on the street. I don't want to be seen, so I creep along walls and slouch through backyards. Across the street from the car I wait until I'm sure no one is around before I slip across to drive away with my lights off. I park about three blocks away, out of sight from my office. Back at the building, I pee in the bushes outside the side entrance. By the time I get back to sleep, there's only another forty-five minutes before it's time to get up, fold my cot, say hi to Luke and go out for breakfast.

On Saturday morning I decide to sleep in. What the hell? At about ten o'clock there's a knock at my door and I feel a jolt of fear. I creep quietly to the door and listen. Maybe some it's some student, knocking on the off chance that I might be in here working.

"It's me," Syndi says, "I know you're in there."

I open the door and peek around her, pulling her in. I shut the door and lock it with a finger pressed to my lips.

"My God. It's hot in here. And it smells. What have you got in here?"

I hadn't even noticed that it was so hot. Now that I think about it, neither air-conditioning nor heat has ever worked in my office. I realize that as I stand in my jockey shorts, I'm coated in a light film of sweat. I look over at the cabinet and see that the doors have been blown open by the gas from my sweaty gym clothes when I moved the cot.

"You don't live at your cabin," she says. "You live here."

I have nothing to say.

"I've come to tell you," she's crying now, "that you're getting what you want. I'm leaving. I'm going back home. I may go to grad school or try to get a job at the Toledo Art Institute.

I try to appear sad about this news. I tell her that this is probably for the best. She's worried about me. Says she feels responsible for ruining my life. I try to dispel this notion because I know it actually is not true.

I *am* sad, watching from my window as she drives away in her piece of shit consolation prize of a car.

I spend most of Saturday doing research in the

library and playing basketball. These activities take my mind off my situation, at least until I return to my office. I go out in the evening for some bar-hopping. I get into a game of darts with some kid who's down from Ohio visiting friends. By the time I hit the cot, I'm pleasantly drunk and ten bucks richer.

I'm startled out of a deep sleep at 4 AM, by pounding on my office door.

"Mr. Roberts?"

It's a deep male voice. *Mr. Roberts* it says. Not Dr. Roberts. I'm resigned to the inevitable.

"Just a minute," I say groggily.

I put on pants and a shirt and open the door to two campus security officers. One says nothing but walks in to start poking around at stuff. My cot is plainly visible. The open sleeping bag that is my only cover, is thrown back onto the lower half of the cot.

"So, Mr. Roberts," the other cop who appears to be about fourteen says, "you're using your office as an apartment?"

"Yeah sort of. I guess. I . . .I'm getting a divorce and I didn't have anyplace else to go."

"Well, sir, you can't stay here. It's not safe. You're going to have make suitable living arrangements. The university never intended for these offices to be used as residences."

"Yes sir," I mumble. I'm completely humiliated. I feel like a criminal of the first order. A loser. A trespasser.

The second cop is smirking. They clearly love this. They've solved a little mystery to which they've devoted many man-hours. Also, they must love breaking me down. They've driven the well-compensated, well-educated badger from his tunnel.

"You have a nice evening, sir," the cherubic law enforcer tells me as they close the door behind them.

I'm confused, groggy—still a bit drunk. They say I can't stay here but they tell me to have a nice evening. I leave the office to walk to my car. I drive out to the rest stop on the interstate and try to get some sleep in the bucket seat that reclines to a not quite prone position.

On Sunday I'm back in the office. Between short, distracted attempts to write a paper that I am scheduled to deliver at the annual conference in San Antonio, I devise a plan to beat the cops at their little game. By standing on the sink I can climb up into the ceiling. I pull the panel back over and fit it into its track—covering my trail. The lights from the hallway are adequate to see what I'm doing up here. I make my way along the concrete block walls, from one office partition to another. If I step onto any of the panels, I'll fall straight through, but as long as I stick to the walls I am completely supported. There's just enough space between my location and the poured concrete floor of the next level, to allow a crouching position. I open a panel and drop down into the hallway. After replacing it, I walk back into my office and look around. There is no evidence that I had just disappeared through the ceiling.

I drive to the home improvement store.

That night I park my car in a new place. The sleeping bag fits nicely onto the boards I lay across the supporting walls in the ceiling. When the officers come up to my floor, I hear the elevator's electronic female voice, announce the floor to which it has delivered them. They knock at my door and wait about thirty seconds before entering with a pass-key. Satisfied that I have found other living arrangements, I hear them close and lock the door.

As usual, I awake at about 3:30 needing to relieve myself. I make my way along the wall system to the bathroom, but before I drop down, I hear once again, the copulating couple in the still-life room. I crouch above it listening until they finish. They talk quietly but I recognize the

Spiderhole

voices. It's Tobias, the department chair and Adrian, one of the advanced painting students.

On Monday, Tobias calls me into his office.

"Listen, Dave," he starts, reluctantly, "the campus cops came to see me."

I say nothing.

"They've been . . . well . . .following you. They say you keep moving your car from place to place."

"There's a law against that?"

"Well, they say you've been sleeping in your office. You know, I don't care. I know you've had a hard time lately. They tell me that it has gone no further than this office, but if it keeps up they will file a report. Now, I don't really know what that would mean. But, I guess what I'm saying is that you should be aware of possible outcomes—if you get my meaning."

I consider telling him what I know of his activities, but it would be a little difficult to explain that I am hovering above him in the ceiling listening to him fucking Adrian, so I sheepishly thank him and return to my office.

After a few undetected weeks of my new home in the ceiling, I'm haunted by the possibilities of the spaces I inhabit. Even, during normal working hours I spend all my free time there. I want to become intimate with the upper reaches of my place of employment. I install an elaborate network of planks that crisscross the walls, pipes, conduits, fixtures, vents. A Viet Cong insurgent, I crawl on my belly—elbows and knees squirm along my wooden highways. I think of using my stealthy network to seek revenge. My enemy is the system, the infrastructure of the university, the campus police. During the workday, after my duties have been adequately performed, I spend my time spying—listening. I know everything that goes on here. I eavesdrop on telephone conversations above Tobias' office before I move on to the student lounge, classrooms—other offices.

There must be opportunities here that had never occurred to me. At night after Denny's, I investigate the campus at large. Sure enough—tunnels. I find an entry point by prying open a metal door in the side of the amphitheatre. It smells of damp concrete. The height of the ceiling varies, depending on the number of overhead pipes. Sometimes water-filled depressions in the floor block my progress. I don't know how deep but I wade through, expecting to be suddenly submerged. Other tunnels branch off to different buildings. In the daylight I try to visualize my underground position. Which branch will take me under the campus thoroughfare to the office of Public Safety? What can I do to them? Poison gas, stink bomb? Water balloon attack?

Back in the ceiling, I work on my out charts and battle plans. One night I decide to drop down into the women's bathroom to relieve myself. A new thrill of sorts. It's a new and unfamiliar world in there. Instead of the blue tiles of the men's room, this bathroom is done in sort of Caucasian flesh tones. I slip into one of the stalls and get an adrenaline rush when I see a bloody mess and a slippery discharge covering much of the toilet. Then I notice a movement from the paper towel chute under the dispenser. Wrapped in bloody paper towels is a still-breathing newborn. I make my way back through the ceiling and down into my office where I dress and hurry by way of the hall itself, back to the women's bathroom. I do the best job I can of cleaning up the viscous mess. I pack all the paper towels into one of the garbage bags I use to take my dirty clothes to the Laundromat. I clean the baby and wrap her in a gym towel.

Whose, I wonder? Adrian? She never appeared pregnant.

I consider keeping her, raising her as my own in the crawl spaces of this public institution. But I think better of it and place her in a hand-made basket that I use for stashing art-show catalogs. Bought it on vacation in Jamaica with Jenny. I remember following the proprietor back into the dark recesses of his little shop to pay for it, where out of my wife's sight, the Rastafarian shopkeeper had secretly sold me a small stash of ganja as well as the basket.

    Is there any way, I wonder, that this newborn could be used as a weapon against the system? Maybe an embarrassment to the establishment. A hostage. I could demand a ransom from Tobias or the police. But I can't come up with anything to make that plan plausible. I don't want to lose the upper hand that I have worked so hard to establish. I've got the high ground, like the Union army on Cemetery Ridge; I'm dug into a defensible position, waiting for Pickett's Charge.

    Back out in the night with my bundle, I drive up and down the streets near campus, looking for a suitable home for little Angela. I pick out a large old Victorian with a nice wooden porch. I park down the block and return to the house. I put the bundle next to the door, ring the bell twice and hurry back to the bushes across the street. I watch as lights come on upstairs. Finally, a man comes to the door, first peeking out the side windows then out into the street, before at last looking down to discover his new treasure.

    Back in my office, I see once again, the flashing blue lights, this time in the vicinity of the Victorian house on Oak Street. I climb back to my nest in the ceiling. I can't sleep now so I watch late night television on the tiny battery-powered Casio I picked up from the pawn shop at the Greyhound Station. It's an expose' about crack cocaine—the scourge it has become—the lives it ruins. I turn the TV off and think about where I might be able to score some.

    The next day I decide to ask Adrian if she knows anybody who can get me some crack. I watch her carefully for tell-tale signs that she has been up to something, but other than the look she gives me about my crack inquiry, nothing jumps out at me. She stares at me through her harsh black-outlined eyes. Her pink hair is, as always, distracting.

"I don't know," she says, "but I can get you some oxycontin."

I've heard of that. Maybe it will be just as good.

She explains how you either crush it up and snort it or melt it in a spoon and shoot up.

Two days later in my little nest in the ceiling, I snort the *hillbilly heroin* and watch Dave Letterman. He's never been funnier. I've never been happier. Afterward, I resume work on my charts and subterranean battle strategies.

Jim Joyce

"Why don't you come on over for a beer? The game comes on in ten minutes."

"I can't," Randy says. "We're having some people over tonight and I gotta help out around the house."

"Who is it?" Dale asks.

"Nobody you know," Randy lies. "Some of Connie's friends from work."

"Aw, come on, man. This game is huge!"

"I can't. You'll see. When you and Jamie tie the knot, things are gonna change. You won't be so independent."

"There's this guy," Dale says, "businessman—Type-A—has a heart attack."

"Listen," Randy says, "I don't have time for this. I can see the point you're gonna make already. Besides, I've heard it before."

***

The hiss, and rattle from the kitchen cause Randy Petersen to reassess the open design of his new house. He cranks up the volume on the final 3:25 of Duke-Carolina. He knows he should be doing more to help out instead of sitting in front of the TV on his fat ass. It's only a regular season game. It doesn't really matter in the big picture. Still …

He detects a movement to the left of the television.

"Listen, I need you to make a grocery run for me."

"Mmmm. Can't I just watch the rest of this game? I'll go as soon as it's over."

Connie moves in to inspect the little box in the upper right corner of the screen.

"Three minutes left," his wife points out. "You know how these things drag out when they start fouling. Our guests will be here in about an hour and I'm still cooking. Then I have to shower and put on my face. You can't just sit there while I do all the work. They're your friends too, you know."

"Hey! I cleaned the house and took out the trash. I even emptied the cans in the bathrooms."

Connie's laser-vision burns through his line of sight to the television, nullifying the significance of the game.

"Do you want some kind of medal?" she asks.

"Yeah, a medal would be nice ... Oh, all right."

He grabs his wallet, pats himself down for car keys. "I know you've told me several times, but who is it that we're having over?"

She taps a malicious foot.

"Barbara and Chris and ..."

"Oh yeah, Ron and his new boyfriend. What's his name?"

"Simon."

"Right, Simon."

He snatches the list of ingredients and the keys Connie dangles. The grocery is only five minutes away if traffic's not too bad—but he'll never make it back in time. It'll take at least five minutes to find each item.

Oregano, marshmallows (the little ones), Parmesan cheese (the block not the pre-shredded), Philadelphia Cream Cheese (Lite). No substitutes!

At the store, he hits the jackpot. Oregano is right there in plain sight, in the little plastic container above the produce, just like she said. He tosses it in his basket. But it takes several trips up and down aisles to find the proper marshmallows.

What does she need them for anyway? What kind of gourmet cook needs little marshmallows?

The game's probably over by now.

Parmesan cheese.

There's a whole rack of the shredded stuff. Maybe that will do. No, better find the block kind. She'll just send him back. It must be here somewhere.

Oh, man! Look at these two. Roommates? Sisters? The tall one smiles at him. Does that mean something?

He sucks in his stomach, smiles back. He palms the list. The list is a dead give-away. Dale' joke about the hen-pecked husband comes to the surface of his consciousness. Only hen-pecked types are sent out with a list.

He lucks into the block Parmesan and needs only the cream cheese to complete his assignment but he trails along behind the two girls, admiring the view. The tall one is wearing a top that falls considerably short of covering her mid-section, dropping straight down from the swell of her breasts. To ease his hand under that gap would be so simple, so right. Her shorts, made of some unidentifiable soft fabric, are so brief that they fail to conceal the most southerly region of her bottom. At last he separates himself from the intentionally provocative display. He fumbles his way unsuccessfully through the interrogation of the self-checkout robot. Eventually, a cashier comes to his rescue, canceling out his failed attempt and pressing a few buttons for him. The machine thanks him and offers its sincere wish that he have a nice day.

On the way home, he's ambushed by a scintillating flash of iridescent blue. He checks the rear view mirror.

The new Z4.

He turns the car around and pulls into the dealership. Maybe he can manage a quick look-see and still make his getaway before one of the salesmen descends upon him. But he lingers a bit too long over the tight fit of the convertible top, backing up to admire the near-ugly bug-face of the grill.

He sees the salesman advancing on him from his periphery. Too late. He's caught. "Dylan McGinnis."

Randy reaches to shake.

Dylan McGinnis is tall, thin and elegant. He also appears to be straight off the plane from New Delhi or Islamabad.

"James Joyce," Randy tells him. He immediately regrets his choice. He should have been Romaleo Joyce or Scooter Joyce, but he was never quick enough on his feet for more than one syllable.

"So, Mr. Joyce, can we put you in this little honey

today?"

Dylan McGinnis, or whatever his real name is, speaks English at him with accentless perfection.

"Actually, I'm just looking today. I … I'm sort of comparison-shopping. You know, I have to think about which car suits my personality. Also, I'm in kind of a hurry and …"

"Well, Mr. Joyce … is it OK if I call you Jim?"

"Uh … James."

"James it is. So I guess you're looking at the TT and the little Porche, right?"

"Right."

"Well, I think you'll find that this little sweetheart compares favorably. Let me just get the keys and we'll take her for a spin."

"Well I …"

But before he can stop Dylan McGinnis, the eager young salesman disappears through the doors of the dealership. Beyond the reflective glass he can make out Dylan at the desk, retrieving the keys, probably explaining that he's got a live one.

"So," Dylan says, handing him the keys, "You got a trade?"

Randy nods toward his four-door, tan Olds Cierra.

Dylan gives him a knowing grimace of pity.

"Give me your keys and I'll have my manager look over your car while we're out. I'm sure we can give you top dollar."

"OK, well just a sec. I have to get my jacket out of the car."

He remembers the Reuger 9mm he keeps under the seat. He grabs the gun and shoves it into the pocket of his nylon jacket. Walking back to the salesman, he tries to hide the weight and bulge of the weapon, holding his elbow tightly to his side.

In the Z, Randy adjusts the leather seat, and the

rear view mirror. Dylan watches his movements from outside the car, explaining the various features. He shows him how to put the top down, how to adjust the stereo speakers' bass and treble.

"Oh, I almost forgot," the salesman says. "We have a little gift for anyone who is—you know—serious, and takes a test drive. I'll be right back."

Randy busies himself with the intricacies of the shimmering toy and barely notices Dylan's sprint back into the dealership. The salesman returns with a baseball cap. It's a jazzy little item with an extra long leather bill. Its sides are slabs of blue that match the car. In the center is a broad section of black extending from the leather bill to the leather adjusting-strap in back. The tiny letters, BMW have been tastefully embroidered in a semi-circle above the rear strap and the circular emblem of the Bavarian Motor Werks, appears at the front of the cap.

"It's yours to keep."

Randy adjusts his new cap in the rear view mirror.

"Actually, there's a whole line of apparel that we can order for you. The jacket's really nice," Dylan says.

Randy imagines pulling into his slot at Harrison High—imagines putting the top up under the admiring gaze of students and colleagues. They watch him unzip his jacket and reach into the passenger seat for his briefcase—watch him adjust his cap. He can almost hear that hot little Monica Sanford, ignoring all the young studs always sniffing around her, purring to him to take her for a spin.

"Go up to the light and take a left onto 52," Dylan says, snapping him out of his wetdream. "The traffic clears a few miles up where it gets curvy and you can air it out a bit."

His hand rests, poised for action on the sporty short-thrust shifter as he leans into the curves.

"Don't touch the brakes," Dylan commands. "The

suspension is perfect. The only time you really need those brakes is when you pull this baby into the garage."

He doesn't want to admit to Dylan that he doesn't have a garage.

Still, at every turn he is tempted to obey his natural instincts born of years behind the wheels of personality-less sedans, protector of wife and kids, always following a safe distance behind the car ahead. He still has the Polite Driver T-shirt, a present from Connie and the kids.

He fights the urge to lift his foot—to brake at every turn. The feel is exhilarating. It's something he had never thought about before. You have to make a conscious effort not to brake.

"So," Dylan says, "what do you do, James?"

Randy starts to answer but Dylan cuts him off.

"Wait! Let me guess. You're a teacher."

"Yeah."

"English?"

"Nope. Math."

"Married?"

Randy holds up his ring hand.

"Kids?"

"Yep."

"Boy and a girl."

"Yep."

"The girl's in college. Boy's in a rock band," Dylan suggests.

"Other way around. What about you? If you don't mind my saying so, you don't look Scottish."

"What? Oh, the name. I made it up. Looks good on a résumé. My real name's Vijay Lopsang, but don't tell anybody. My mother is Indian and my father was Sherpa. Killed in an avalanche on Kangchenjunga. My mother married a computer programmer and we moved to California when I was six."

"Kang … ju …"

"Kangchenjunga. Still never been climbed."

"And your stepfather ... he's Scottish?"

"Nah, he's Indian too, from Madras. Like I said, I just made the name up."

"And this is your ambition? Car salesman?"

Vijay Lopsang gives James Joyce a look.

"I just built a new house. Paid cash. Up in the eastern hills—pool, garden with a water feature—ten plus acres."

"Ok, I didn't mean to insult you. Say, what do *you* drive, Dylan?"

"Didn't you see it? That sweet little red and black chromy thing parked by the front door that all those guys were standing around."

"You mean the Harley?"

"Fake Harley."

"So what is it really?"

"It's a Honda, of course. Take a left here." Dylan points to a road that leads up into the hills. "Most reliable vehicles on the planet. I gotta know I'm gonna actually make it to work every day. You should hear it though. Sounds like the real thing, but without the vibration and oil leaks. As soon as I got 'er home I put on a set of Vance and Hines pipes."

"So," Randy/James says, "Are *you* married?"

Dylan/Vijay holds up his ringless left hand. "Girlfriend."

"Got her picture in your wallet?"

"Don't carry a wallet," Dylan says, extracting a roll of bills held in place with a rubber band. "Wallets are so *last week*." He winks and puts the wad back in his pocket. "You've probably seen her though. She's in that Budweiser commercial. You know, the one where the three fat guys fill up the pool and wait for something to happen and these three babes show up. She's the brunette."

Randy can't remember which one she is but feels a

twinge of jealousy. He thinks about Connie. She's put on a few pounds lately but he never lets on that it's a problem.

"Do you think this dress makes me look fat?"

Suddenly, on the curvy road, he feels the discomfort of his seatbelt rubbing, pressing something hard into his side. He reaches into his jacket pocket and without thinking, extracts the Rueger. Dylan immediately loses his cheerful animation—becomes quiet.

"Look," Dylan says, "I don't care about the car. Take it. I just work there. It's no skin off my teeth."

Randy considers the offer. At first he has no intention of doing anything like what Dylan must be imagining. But the day has turned in an unexpected direction. He could just keep on driving or hold the salesman for some kind of ransom. They'd come after him with police cars and helicopters. He wouldn't go down without a fight though. In the end they'd trap him up in the hills. If he could make the high country he could hold them off for hours. They'd bring Connie in. Put her on the bull-horn to talk him down. But ...

"Sorry," Randy says. "I just keep this for protection. I had to pull it out of the car before your guys checked it out. Listen, hadn't we better be getting back?"

Randy sees a wave of relief pass over Dylan's face.

"So, is it loaded?"

"Well, what good would it do to carry around an unloaded gun?"

"I mean, do you have a permit and all?"

"Nah. Wanna hold it?"

Dylan just stares at the gun.

Randy passes it to him.

"Don't worry. The safety's on."

Dylan accepts it gingerly, balancing the piece in his hand.

"Feels good, doesn't it? Ever fire one?"

Dylan shakes his head.

"Want to?"

"Sure."

"I know this road," Randy says. "It winds up into those rocks. We could go up there, pop off a couple rounds and get out before anybody calls the cops."

Dylan checks his watch, looks at Randy's eager face.

"OK," he says. "You're on."

***

Randy shows him how to steady the Rueger with both hands. Before he fires off a round, Dylan crouches swinging from side to side, brandishing his new weapon like a TV crimebuster.

"You're not ready for all that," Randy says. "Just aim it and see if you can hit that beer can." He points to one of the many articles of trash that lovers have pitched, along with used condoms, from their midnight parking places.

Dylan takes aim and fires. A plume of dust rises about two feet to the left of the can.

"You closed your eyes. Keep your eyes open and squeeze. You don't *pull* the trigger. You squeeze."

Dylan fires again. This time the plume is only inches away from the target can. The next round sends it spinning.

"We'd better get out of here," Randy says.

But Dylan is in a zone. Randy recognizes the look. The power of the weapon, traveling up his hand to his brain, has mesmerized him. He squeezes off round after round until only a hollow click blends with the ringing in their ears.

"Wow!" Dylan says. "Where'd you get it? Like a gun show or something? I hear it's really hard these days."

"Nah. I got it from this woman—a friend of a friend—said she didn't *need* it any more."

Dylan raises his eyebrows.

Randy shrugs.

"OK. Now let's vamoose," Randy says.

"You'd better let me drive," Dylan says. "We've been gone quite a while. They begin to worry sometimes, back at the dealership. You never know when you might get a crazy."

Dylan lifts his eyebrows as if to say 'know what I mean?'

"Besides, you showed me something. Let me show you something."

Dylan handles the *Z* like a pro, zigging and zagging down the hill at high speed. Before they rejoin the main road, they hear the electric whoop of sirens heading toward them. They wave, real friendly-like as the cop car passes them on its way up the hill.

***

Back at the dealership, the other salesmen watch Dylan and Randy, standing back to admire the now dusty little roadster. A heavy man in a dark suit approaches the two, extends his hand.

"Big Jake," the man says. "Friends call me Big'n."

"Hi, Ran … James," Randy says.

"So wadya think?" the new guy says.

They're sending in the big guns now.

"It's nice. I'll have to think about it."

"Our boy here can really handle one of these." The big man clamps Dylan on the shoulder. "Listen …"

"James."

"Listen, Jim. We've got somebody pretty hot to trot on this particular car but I haven't heard from him today and it's getting late. Says he's working on financing. But I'll tell you what. It's the end of the month and I really need to move some product. What would it take to put you in the cockpit of this little rocket today?"

Randy feels the weight of the Rueger in his jacket. His previously semi-automatic inspired self-assurance is gone now, drained away with the emptied clip.

"I ... I don't know. I need more time."

Dylan is clearly fading into the background now. Randy is disappointed that the salesman seems to play no further part in these negotiations. They had shared a moment. But now Dylan backs away toward his Honda. His part in this is over.

The big guy lays a chubby pink hand on Randy's shoulder. The power play makes him feel small and child-like. He wishes his gun were loaded. He'd just feel so much more confident. He'd say 'I'll think about it. I'll get back to you,' instead of what he actually finds himself saying.

"I'll have to talk it over with my wife."

Now there is an issue. His wife. There will certainly be trouble. He'll have to think of something. He was in a wreck. No that's no good, unless he intentionally wrecks the Cierra now. Maybe he witnessed a wreck and helped the injured driver.

"Sure," the manager says. "I see how it is. I can see you're the responsible type. Probably just wanted a little thrill for the day, eh? Little joyride? That's OK. Not everybody is cut out for the Z4."

He joins Randy in a sigh directed at his tan four-door sedan. He looks unblinkingly into Randy's eyes, sandwiching his hand in both of his. "Listen, why don't you stop in next Monday and ask for me?"

He hands Randy his card.

Randy frees his eyes from the manager's long enough to read the name. *Big Jake Swindle.* A drawing on the card shows a tiny family, encircled by the protective arms of Big'n.

"We've got a new Hyundai coming in. They're really pretty nice now. Not like they used to be ... heh,

heh. Consumer Reports puts 'em right up there with the Japs. This one's a sweet little four-door—tan I think—or off-white. Perfect for a guy like you. I hear they're still a little underpowered, but they've made 'em very *safe*."

Big Jake Swindle gives Randy his smarmiest smile.

"Listen, I gotta go now. You have a real nice day and ...oh yeah ... keep the hat." Big'n chucks him on the shoulder.

Before getting into his tan Cierra, Randy stops to say goodbye to Dylan. They chat for a minute about the bike, but Dylan seems distracted. He can't seem to tear his eyes from the magazine he's engrossed in. The bond they had established on the winding test drive has been broken by his wimpy inability to deliver at crunch time.

Randy asks Dylan to fire up the bike so he can hear the Vance and Hines pipes. Dylan disinterestedly obliges him. The machine rumbles to life and throbs pleasingly. Randy lays his hand on the tank, allowing the pulse and rumble, to churn his testosterone to its previous Z-and-gunplay-inspired level.

***

Randy turns his sluggish, suspensionless Cierra onto his own street. His car, he now recognizes, is sluggish and suspensionless. He's aware of every squeak as it squishes around each turn. He glances over his shoulder into the back seat.

Nothing.

The groceries are gone. He stops the car, gets out and searches behind the seats, under them, looks in the trunk. He turns the car around and heads back to the grocery.

What's the point? The guests—who were they again—Chris and ... and ... Ron? They must have come and gone by now. He passes the two girls from the grocery store. At least they look like the same ones. They must live in the neighborhood. The tall one—the brunette—is now enveloped in a kind of silvery space suit. They rollerblade gracefully toward him in slo-mo. Their inside arms are interlocked while the outside arms swing freely, keeping pace with their fluid swim.

Must be lesbos.

But instead of continuing on to the grocery, he turns back in at the dealership. He'll be a man. Why should he have to ask permission if he wants to make a deal? What if it is foolish? He's paid his dues. Big deal. Fuck Chris and Ron and Ron's boyfriend and Connie and …and … oh yeah … Barbara. Fuck Barbara too.

He fondles the *Z*'s convertible top again. This time no one comes to pester him. Where's a salesman when you need one? He enters the showroom where Dylan sits on a desk in his leather jacket, leafing through a gun magazine. Surely he's seen him out there.

Dylan lifts his eyes for a second before continuing to flip pages.

"Hey. I'm back. I've decided I want to deal."

"Bring a permission slip from home, did ya?"

Dylan and makes a motion like the cracking of a whip, releasing as he does so, a *w h o o s h a c k* sound from his lips.

Some cool liquid that has remained until this moment, pooled at the viscous lake-bottom of Randy's narrowed eyes, floats to the surface. He pats at the lump of cold steel in his jacket, remembering sadly that Dylan had returned it to him in a condition that would allow it to serve only as a hammer. But he can see in Dylan's eyes that the young man recognizes a danger here… that he may be about to unleash something better left harnessed in the mild-mannered family man.

"Look at this," Dylan says, trying to diffuse the James Joyce Bomb. He shows Randy the full-page ad in his gun magazine. The Glock semi-automatic 9mm model 17 with Trijicon sight.

"Nice piece," Randy says. "Say, you ever see Taxi Driver?"

"Part of it. I was channel surfing and came across it. Too slow for me."

"You should rent it. Besides everything's too fast these days. Slow can be good."

Randy suddenly remembers what he's here for.

"Anyway I came to deal. So lets deal."

"Too late," Dylan says glumly. "Mr. Swindle's gone home for the day."

"I don't care about Mr. Fucking Swindle. I want to make my deal with you."

"There's not much I can do without the boss," Dylan says, brightening, "but come on back and we can at least work up some figures."

Randy follows Dylan down a depressingly clean, well-lighted and cheerful hallway, adorned with posters of nearly every model of Corvette ever made. In a little office that contains nothing but a desk, a calculator and a computer, Randy takes a seat opposite Dylan.

Randy begins the negotiations by sliding the Rueger 9mm across the desk.

"This is part of my trade," he explains, "along with the car."

***

Randy turns for a second time onto his own street. It's dark now. He leans to check his look in the mirror. He adjusts his cap. He's wearing it backward now so the wind can't catch the long bill and lift it away. As he approaches his house he notices three figures standing on the lighted front steps. A cop car sits in front of the house. Connie must have filed a missing person. She's talking to the two uniforms and gesturing. She clamps one hand to her forehead. One of the cops jots down notes.

Lakeview Motel

Randy pulls up behind the cruiser with a subtle, throaty roar that causes the cops and Connie to look. He dismounts and shoves the kickstand into place with his foot. He wipes quickly at the blemish left by his inexperienced boot-heel where it accidentally brushed the tank as he swung his leg over. He walks up the steps toward his door, fighting the urge to look back at the machine. Each step produces a leathery squeak from his new jacket and pants, all part of his deal with Dylan. As he rehearses the opening lines of his lame explanation, he notices the cops looking on with envy at his new ride.

He's anxious to get this over with so he can sit down with a vodka tonic and study the gun magazine now rolled under his arm. He's eager to familiarize himself with every attribute of his next purchase, the Glock semi-automatic 9mm model 17—with Trijicon sight.

The High Ground

"Why do you go there? Why would you want to spend the holidays all alone?" Felicia asks. "Oh, wait," she says. "I know. It's because you *have* the place. You spent all that time and money to build it and by God, you're going to get your money's worth."

"You've got me figured out," I say.

I decide to let it go at that. Felicia's my best friend.

She thinks she knows everything about me—like what's going on in my head, even. But I keep some things to myself, like my feelings of guilt and disappointment at how I've turned out. She thinks we both have good careers. We're successful, respectable people. She doesn't recognize my failure. That's because she hasn't been burdened with the expectations of a famous father hanging over her like an unsteady tower of crushed Buicks.

My sister and I used to watch him through the keyhole. We were forbidden to enter that sacred space from 10:00 AM until 5:00 PM when he "got off work." Sometimes we saw him typing, but much of the time he read or even slept in there, leaning back in his barber chair, the one he bought from Clarence's son after the old barber passed on. Surrounded by his books and his testosterone world of oak and leather, his hair and beard grew out long and white after Clarence died.

This room was his life. He never stooped to teaching.

"The easy way out," he said. "The coward's way of bypassing sacrifice. Oh, I see them on Thursdays down at the Black Bull," he said to my mother, "in their corduroy jackets with their leather patched sleeves and their little salt and pepper Van Dykes, pulling at their Guinnesses, pretending to be a part of *my* world—of *our* world," he said, to me this time, lowering a despotic paw to my shoulder.

This was my charge. It was up to me to take over the family business, to resurrect his giant shadow in my own contour.

I remember the day I gave him the news. I knocked on his door, timidly at first, then with more force. He never acknowledged the timid knocker. If it was important enough to warrant a disturbance before 5:00 PM "it's important enough for a decent pounding."

"Come," he said.

When his tyrannical voice boomed from behind that door I almost peed my pants. I had hoped, when I told him of my appointment to a position at the university, he would ease up; that he'd see it as a success story. After all, I was no stellar pupil. It had, in fact, crossed my mind that the reason I got the position may have been because of my impressive surname rather than my mediocre credentials. Still, weren't college professors the people we were supposed to look up to? Weren't they the mentors who molded young minds into minds like his? Instead, he slammed the book he was reading down on the arm of his chair and ordered me out of his sight. Then he locked the door.

When five o'clock rolled around, he poured his usual scotch and soda and the subject never came up again, unless from the lips of some dinner guest who innocently asked me about my work. On those occasions my father would listen politely to my answer before continuing with his exposition over his newest book or his disgust with the New York Times best-seller list.

"They're only *best sellers* because they are marketed *by* idiots *to* idiots—and— idiots are so abundant."

For my birthday that year, he bought me a tan corduroy jacket with leather patches.

Was it his disappointment in me that sent him to an early grave?

Felicia is perfectly happy with her university job. She gives papers on Feminist Anality, her area of expertise, at the MLA conference. I haven't figured out what Feminist Anality is yet, but I always nod as though I comprehend. This week she'll be moderating a panel on Queer Theory at Swarthmore.

That's enough for her. She doesn't have this famous ghost burning at her from the heavens with his disapproving off-planet gaze. Still, despite her national recognition, our department chair won't allow her to start her program in Queer Theory unless she modifies the title.

The board of regents doesn't like the sound of it.

"It's vulgar," they say.

"So when are you leaving?" she asks over her vodka tonic and cigarette. She blows smoke from the side of her mouth like Lauren Bacall. She only smokes when she's out for an evening of drinking. You can tell she's not an accomplished smoker. She's way too dramatic about it.

"I'm flying out tomorrow at 6:40."

"AM?"

I nod.

"Yuck. But if you need a ride to the airport, I can take you."

"Thanks, but I don't want to do that to anybody. I'm taking a cab."

I can tell she's relieved; but it was nice of her to offer.

It always feels strange to be back here. When I left in August, the mountains were brown except for one tiny patch of snow in a north-facing gully high on the peaks.

I always expect something bad—broken windows, vandalism, theft or worse—burned to the ground maybe. So far there has only been normal deterioration. One year a section of deck-railing was down. Two times now, I've had to replace the toilet when it froze and cracked, but nothing major.

I cup my hands to peek in the small window in the front door. Around front, I inspect the big arc of window for damage but—nothing. At last I unlock the door and enter my time capsule. I always think of the party that came across Scott's Antarctic hut. The frying pan on the stove still contained pieces of fifty-year-old frozen blubber. Unopened blue and orange Huntley & Palmers Biscuit tins, tins of baking powder and cocoa. They're still there to this day. You could open them, thaw out that piece of blubber and start dinner. There must have been moments

Highground

when Scott wished he had never set out for the Pole. Long after his death, everything in his little hut remained as he had left it, preserved by the dry cold and the isolation of the place, waiting for his return.

My cabin is isolated as well, but in a much more civilized way. You can, for instance, drive right up to it. Once inside, you can turn on electricity, fire up the well pump, clean up the thousands of dead flies, pour yourself a drink and read the paper.

Looking around, I relive the last moments before I left. Here's the newspaper from the little town in the valley below. It's from last August. *Commissioners reluctant to fund beaver dam eradication* on page 2. On page 16, *Trustees make town hall smoke free*.

My last cigar butt sits in a disgusting cereal bowl of ashes on the electric range. (I never did buy an ashtray.) In the bedroom, the calendar still reads June. Dates are circled with notes written below them: Jun 22, airport, Jun 30, airport again. My sister's visit. On the refrigerator there's a picture of the two of us standing triumphantly on the summit of Mount Massive. If it weren't for the twenty other day-hikers behind us placing cell phone calls, you'd think we had just scaled the Lhotse Face.

Satisfied with my inspection, I notice that the feeling of strangeness, of suspended time—has passed—and that I am once again in the present. Already, the things I carried in from the rental car have begun to replace the past with the here and now. On the table sits my new laptop. I still have my old one. It's back home in a heap of electronic refuse that I don't know what to do with—other old computers, scanners, hard drives, outdated storage devices. Are these items—mostly still functioning—too good to dispose of or too useless to keep lying around?

Staring at the computer, I think about our culture of disposable diapers, dinnerware, acres of automobile tires that refuse to decay. Back home in my small college town, big corporations abandon their Wal-Marts or multipurpose hardware/lumber mega-stores only to move across the by-pass into a bigger version of the same shoddy, design-free construction, leaving the old one to sit idle or to pass through a decade of transformations from specialty discount outlet, to flea-market, to its final manifestation as pile of disintegrating metal much like the current state of my electronic rubbish heap. By the time that happens, the company has outgrown its new location and leaves *it* to a similar fate.

Maybe I'll write about that.

That's why I'm here after-all. My get-away. My silent retreat, free of the world's distractions—where I can think. I'll stockpile food, liquor and cigars. A mountain man. A lone wolf. Like Scott at the South Pole.

I see my story.

On his lunch hour the Wal-Mart manager, a fat man with a cherubic Christian face, crosses the by-pass to the old store, now a flea market. "See ya later, Chrissy," he says to his current chubby Christian-looking management-trainee. "Hold down the fort."

"Right, chief. Everything's under control." She mock-salutes him. "I'm leading the motivational meeting at 2:15, remember. Be sure to be back for that."

"Can't wait," he says. He means it. He gets all choked up every time they join hands to sing the company song.

He drives across the street—naturally—nobody in America walks. In his head he recreates the flea mall's prior Wal-Mart life. He pictures the place bustling with happy shoplifters. He experiences a pang of regret that he missed out on that opportunity with Janice, the pretty management trainee who clearly had designs on him.

"So," she'd say, "Is everything all right? At home, I mean. Are you *happily* married?"

She had touched his arm lightly when she asked

this question, her face full of concern. She's in Tulsa now, managing her own store. Or was it Omaha?

Maybe he should call her.

Look. There's his former office, an elevated room with a two-way mirror where he could observe the goings-on of the floor like a mob boss overseeing a casino.

He strolls from booth to booth, searching for a Valentine's gift for his wife. In one of the booths he fingers a few brooches that sit on the antique Queen Anne dining table the proprietor uses for a desk/display table. A pet squirrel hops up on the table. He can tell it's not a wild squirrel because it wears a little red collar. The animal seems to be the sole caretaker of the place, as no human is anywhere in sight. The squirrel investigates him, hopping back and forth, chattering, and at last, ringing a little bell with its paw. The manager hears some feminine laughter and a man's lower pitched murmurings. From behind a curtain—his wife emerges, straightening her skirt.

I see the manager spiraling out of control. He tries to get even by propositioning Chrissy. Chrissy's shocked when he exposes himself. Reports him for sexual harassment. He agrees to attend Wal-Mart sexual harassment counseling, but they fire him anyway. His wife runs off with the flea-man and his squirrel. Unreasonably, he blames Wal-Mart and its policy of reckless acquisition and abandonment of real estate for his wife's infidelity. He burns both properties to the ground.

Then what?

I don't know.

I realize that I'm shivering, daydreaming in a freezing cabin while staring at the object that could warm me. My woodstove is small, the smallest one I could find, but it heats the entire house once you get it going full blast. It's beautiful. I paid extra for its blue-green enameled surface and its glass door. You get all the heat and efficiency of a stove and at least some of the visual solace of a fireplace. But when I open the door, I see the saddest thing.

At first, I think it's an unburned piece of wood. It's a bird. A mountain bluebird, its brilliant hue camouflaged in gray from hours of struggle with the cold ashes of its death chamber. At some point it must have made a decision to give up. The realization that all hope was gone must have come. That was the moment it laid its head on the ledge just behind the glass door like a dog might rest its chin on your lap.

I pick the creature up from where it died looking sadly out into the world, one quarter inch away, and dust away the gray ashes. The blue feathers return to their original iridescence. I wonder when he took his final breath. Two months ago? Or if I had arrived yesterday rather than today, might I have saved him—or her? I feel that I owe the bird something. I'm responsible in a way. I should give it a send-off, a burial. Maybe I'll sing something appropriate.

But I need a fire and the send-off it gets in the end, is a careless toss off the front deck.

I carefully reinstall the water filter and at last I'm ready to turn on the well pump—always a scary moment. It's a two-part procedure: the switch on the electric panel, then the throw-switch on the pump box itself. One year, nothing happened. An electric charge laced with dollar-signs ran through my body.

A dry well?

That well was drilled at great expense, to a depth of 700 feet, twice the distance of the height of the tallest building on our campus. It took me an hour to figure out that I had labeled the throw-switch backwards and was actually turning it off.

This time though, I push the lever and I'm rewarded by the whoosh of water pouring into the system. I'm thrilled with its immediacy; it rushes up instantly from its black tube set deep into the granite earth. I hear its satisfying gurgle as it fills the pressure tank. Water and air mix in all the previously drained pipes. Upstairs, where the faucets and showers are open, microbursts of stinking sulfuric air burble out—but no water. I know enough now to be patient. Even residual amounts of water freeze and expand enough to block the pipes until I can get some warmth in here.

I pour myself a drink and pull up to the heatless fire, still in my coat. As the fire slowly warms me, with Johnny Walker's assistance, I doze. I'm awakened by noises. I forget for a moment where I am. My glass is lying unbroken on the floor in a pool of spilled scotch, along with my book. The sounds, I realize, are from water, now streaming from all the open faucets. I go around closing everything and return to the basement to make one final check before shuttering the complex water system back behind its enclosure. But when I get down there—it's raining. For a moment I stand transfixed as water drizzles steadily from overhead.

It's coming from everywhere—evenly—like a gentle spring shower. The scene is so tranquil that it takes a moment to register that what I'm witnessing is a minor disaster.

I shut down the pump and run back upstairs. My beautiful maple floor is swimming in an inch of water. I have no idea where it has come from. I furiously push-broom water out into the freezing night.

With the pump off, no further water spews into the lakebed of my varnished floor, and in the basement, the rain has abated. But I've got to find the leak, and the only way to do it is to turn the pump back on. I hit the switch and run upstairs. There it is. The dishwasher. I shut the pump down.

Why did I let the real estate guy convince me that I needed such amenities? Resale value? I don't even cook. I eat sandwiches and drink coffee from my single cup, scotch from my single glass. I disconnect the supply tube to the dishwasher, but it's too late. The floor swelling already.

Actually, I wish there were *more* duties that required immediate attention. I see bits of trim that I never finished. Here and there is a wall that really could use repainting.

I'm stalling.

I'm just looking for any excuse to avoid the real work I came here for. About the only decent writing I've done has been here, at the table in the corner, a poor man's imitation of my father's leathery office.

On campus, my writing ambitions are barely recognized. I'm just one of many composition instructors. I show first-year students how to write a business letter, an essay, or the occasional attempt at plebian poetry or short fiction. I *am* a favorite of the campus newspaper's photographer though. My face is well known there—so well known in fact, that many people are embarrassed to be seen with me. Only Felecia seems to not mind.

I'm the spitting image of Adolph Hitler.

My father was the first to point out my resemblance to the dictator. I wasn't too happy with his observation at the time, but after he died, I decided to roll with it. I saw it as my signature mark, like Woody's glasses or Truman's fedora. Still, the similarity might have gone unnoticed if it weren't for the hair-style and mustache I adopted. I just couldn't help myself. I've always found it attractive—and effective. And when I get really fired up about my subject, I grasp both sides of the podium and shake my head violently, causing my hair to fall down over my eyes. I brush it back vigorously with my hand and pound the lectern for emphasis. I don't know why this mustache design has never caught on but I've never seen it on any other contemporary of mine; clipped squarely at both ends, it never interferes with eating or drinking.

Over the next few days, in fits and starts, I poke and prod at my story about the Wal-Mart manager. My father used to wad up pages that didn't meet his standards, as he ripped them from his typewriter. I simply hit the delete button and it's gone, leaving no paper trail. After two days—between drinks and peeing off the deck and staring at the mountains and feeling sorry for myself—I come up with 557 words.

I'm lonely. I call Felicia.

"How's it going?" She asks. "Getting lots done?"

"Oh, yeah. It's great being here. This is what I need. Complete isolation. Freedom to think."

She's distracted. I don't think she's even listening to me. She's just trying to be polite. We were always just friends but I need more from her now.

Maybe I'm in love with her.

As we talk I hear rattling pans, running water. Can't she see I need her undivided attention?

She's making dinner, she tells me, for Roger Cranston, one of the creative writers. I never cared about her interest in the little weasel before. What a dweeb—skinny, bow legged. What does she see in him? Maybe under those size 28 Dockers, he's packing a sch-long Godzilla would envy. Or maybe it's his work. That must be it. He's a better writer than me.

Than I—better writer than I.

I need to know.

"Listen," I say. "Why don't you ask Roger to email me one of his pieces. I'd really like to read it."

"Ok. I think he'll be thrilled that you're interested."

I hear her muffled voice tell Roger about my interest in his crap. She must have her hand over the phone. There's a clatter as she puts it down. More sounds: a sigh and soft music somewhere in the distance. He's probably feeling her up. It's a long time before she comes back on.

Maybe, if his stuff's any good, I can learn something from him. I can borrow some of his ideas in a way that won't be obvious.

When I'm not on the phone, I pace the buckled floor, drinking. Or I watch TV. My satellite dish actually brings in more channels than I get at home. I call the number on the screen to order pay-per-view movies or I watch HBO. It's just for research though. I can borrow and adapt themes I see in the movies.

I spend Sunday watching football. I go for a run but I can't breathe. I never had trouble with the altitude before. But this time I actually have to stop at the slightest incline. I cough and spit. I look down on the snowy road and there in the spittle, I see a tiny fleck of blood. It's probably nothing. I spit again and it's just spit.

I call Felicia. "How'd it go with Roger?"

"I feel fat," is her answer to this question. "You know how skinny he is. I tried to put his pants on, you know, just for kicks. I couldn't get them up over my big lard-ass. I gotta start working out seriously. Do you think I'm fat?"

I can't respond. Suddenly, the thought of Roger with his pants off is so disgusting that I feel sick.

"You're not fat—Felicia?"

"Yeah?"

"Nothing. I gotta go now. I really don't feel too good. I think I'm coming down with something."

It's hard to sleep here. The weight of silence keeps me up. Sometimes I go out on the deck at night just to listen, for anything human. The only evidence of others of my species is the omnipresent drone of jetliners high overhead. In a place less quiet you wouldn't even hear them. At any time of day or night, there's at least one. My solitary outpost is the crossroads of one the busiest air corridors in the world. The New York-LA, Chicago-LA, Seattle-Atlanta, Washington-San Francisco routes, all crisscross over my stovepipe. I've counted as many as seven contrails at one time during the daylight hours. I wonder if I could signal one should the need arise. From my bed I can only see out in one direction. I watch the red taillights blink from one side of the sliding glass balcony doors to the other.

I send an S.O.S out into the stratosphere with my flashlight, but no one comes to check on me.

The sounds that I do hear are maddening. The refrigerator is amplified by contrast with the quiet. I take apart the compressor and fan, reassembling it many times, stuffing extra insulation and rubber grommets in places they were not meant to go, discarding parts that I consider unnecessary—voiding the warranty. I become obsessed with schemes for quieting the thing. I try encasing the entire machine in cardboard and insulation. When this fails, I build a permanent enclosure with its own entrance door.

In the end my solution is to unplug the thing.

I shiver when the coyotes start their howling. The woodstove pops. Wood shifts with a thump. The pot of water on the stove hisses. 2 AM. What's the use? I get up.

I start coughing. I cough so hard that my stomach cramps up on me. I wonder if I should be eating. I pretty much stopped that a few days ago. There are plenty of calories and nutrients in Scotch.

There is a sharp pain in my back. Or is it my side? My chest? Heart attack?

It doesn't go down my arm though. I take a breath. Pain. I've cracked a rib from the high altitude cough. Pulmonary edema.

Get a hold of yourself, man. You've read too many mountain climbing accounts. In the bathroom I cough harder and spit out something. I bend down close to the toilet to get a good look in the dark. Something extraordinary has shot from depths of my lungs like a Mt. St. Helens lava-bomb. With a certain dread, I flip on the light. A big clot of ancient Cabernet Sauvignon blood. It's been in there for a while. It's petrified. I make myself cough again and this time I produce a fresh wad—new blood this time—as cheerfully red as the finish on a new Corvette.

I'm dying.

In the morning I try to convince myself that the blood is from the dry, thin air. My nose always bleeds here. It's probably just running down into my lungs. Is that possible?

By noon I've added 37 new words. Outside now, it's a whiteout. The weather report says we can expect up to two feet.

So what? I've got Scotch.

I call my sister in Ohio but no one answers. I watch my DVD of *The Jerk* for the fifth time. There must be something in it, some spark of an idea that I can use in my story. But just as Navin is reading his sad, melting goodbye note, everything shuts down. The TV is silenced and with one final wheeze, the irritating refrigerator compressor, (I relented and plugged it back in,)—gives up the ghost.

In the hour of computer battery I have left, having no other electronic distractions available to me, I tear though my most productive period of writing since my arrival. Unfortunately, I forget to save the 800 new words as the battery gives out and the screen quickly goes black.

"What?" I shout at the deaf and dumb liquid crystal display, "Where's my warning message?"

I want to call Felicia, but the phone is, I remember now, powered by electricity. My cell phone has never gotten a signal here. I can't even get water because the well pump is also run by electricity. I can't take it here any longer. I need lights, music, noise—people. I pack some

Highground

things and venture out into the storm. It's dark now. Maybe I can get out of here before the snow gets too deep. There's about a foot so far and it's still coming down hard. The rental car has front wheel drive. If I can get it going fast enough, it's mostly downhill to the main highway about five miles from here.

I turn the key.

Nothing.

No dash lights, no radio—nada. I must have left the dome light on. I decide to start walking. It's not terribly cold but the snow is getting deeper all the time. It takes hours to trudge to the highway. What now? At last a car comes and I wave, but he passes me by. Spiraling patterns of snow spin in front of his receding headlight beams. The lights, usually sprinkled throughout the valley, are dark.

Something big has happened—a war maybe—or a terrorist attack.

Finally, a pickup comes along. I stand in the middle of the road and wave frantically. What choice does he have? Surely my desperation shows. He stops for me.

"Bad night to be out walkin'," the guy says. "Hop in."

"What's happened?" I say. "It's something big, right?" I pull back my parka, giving the guy the full force of my Hitleresque face. "I mean—there's no power! Has there been an attack?"

The guy just stares at me.

"What? What are you not telling me?" I shout. I start coughing violently. I feel a wad of something expelled from my open mouth and hear it splat on the seat between us.

The guy looks down at it with big eyes.

"You know, don't you?" I say. I shake my head as I grip the dash and the back of the bench seat. When my hair falls down over my eyes I shove it back as I lean into him. "You know what it is!" I say, my mustache twitching.

He still doesn't say anything. He just keeps on looking at me like I'm off my rocker, like he's seen the devil or something. He pulls over and reaches across me for the door handle. "Get out," he says. Then he adds in a more kindly tone, "Please. I don't want no trouble, mister."

I take a swing at him and connect with the side of his face. He holds his hand up to his mouth and it comes away bloody. He gives me the big eyes again. He knows something. I can tell. But then the guy just jumps out of his own truck and takes off running through the snow. I see him look back once and stumble. He gets to his feet and disappears into the snow-covered sages.

Whatever it is, it's pretty obvious this guy has something to do with it.

I slide over to the driver's seat and take off. It's an hour and ten minutes in good conditions, down the mountain to Pueblo. On the way down, the snow gets lighter. The two feet at the top of the pass begins to taper to about one foot. Still the trip takes me twice as long as usual. By the time I'm down to river level, there's no snow at all and the lights of the city are glowing as brightly as ever. I drive straight to Wal-Mart.

The attack must have come in the high country first. They'll probably spread out to the rest of the continent from there. That's how it works. You have to establish control of the high ground.

In the store I see people going about their business as though nothing has happened and nothing is about to happen. It's good to be in here though. Good to see all these folks. It's warm here.

It's pretty obvious they don't have a clue as to what's going on in the outside world. They'll find out soon enough though, I guess. In the mean time, I'm stocking up for a long siege. I grab toilet paper, cookies, DVD's, coffee filters. I'm buyin' up just about everything I can load into that pickup before there's a big run on supplies. I need a gun. And look at this. They sell refrigerators at Wal-Mart these days. Better get cough drops too.

Land of Many Uses

    They think I'm still asleep, but I just don't want to get up. I'd rather wait for the crash through the door, the leap onto the bed—the *attack of the basement-dweller*.
    A recent study showed teenagers need more sleep than adults. That's what my mom told me. Since she believes in recent studies, she waits until the absolute last minute before she opens the basement door.
    My dad believes in hard work, might-is-right, the American Way. In my eighteen years on the planet he has

directed maybe a hundred words at me. They're usually the same words—*godammit*—my first name, *Alan*—and my middle name—*David.*

Only *he* would call me Alan David.

I've been bad.

I have no retort, no excuses, no explanations for why I forgot to take out the trash, or left his tools out, or stayed out past eleven. But it's not fair. I'm good. Can't he see that? Some of my friends do drugs, drink, have sex, shoplift. Not me.

I might steal his car.

I hear his radio, out there just beyond my closed door. His back is to the sun—the best seat at the breakfast table. I hate his radio station. *Fly me to the Moon*, *Bridge over Troubled Water*, *Moon River*, an instrumental version of *Proud Mary*, Leonard Nemoy singing *Light my Fire.* Soon I'll be out there, opposite him, squinting into the morning sun—the antithesis to his best seat in the house. Pete and Jim don't use words like *antithesis* because they were thinking about sex, drugs, alcohol and shoplifting when we did that one in English. My friend Nancy does though. She's in the debate club.

Soon I'll be answering my mom's questions about the day ahead while I try to use his body to shield my eyes from the glare, ducking and weaving with each mouthful of granola. But I won't get away without one of his lectures. He delivers them to Mom, but that's just his way of speaking to me indirectly. That's *our* way. That's what we've come up with as a method of communication.

"Godammit Alan David," sometimes warrants a response.

"I'm sorry," I say to my mom.

"He knows you're sorry, Hon."

I hear the latch of the basement door, the charge through the house. Nails skid over ceramic tile, oriental carpet ripples as it slides across hardwood. The final corner is turned as rear end slides out from under—then the explosion, as the door slams open into the wall. I cover my head with the bedspread, but Bruce manages to burrow his cold nose under the covers to nuzzle my bare skin.

"All right, all right. I'm getting up."

Mom adores me. I can see this in the way she stands, arms akimbo, watching the touching scene between boy and dog. "Time to get up," she says, sweetly—needlessly.

Dad is tall, angular, keeps himself in shape by working out at the club. Not like the other dads I know. Jim's dad is short and fat, but friendly. He's always in his Lazy-Boy reading the paper or watching TV when I come over. I know he can hear me coming up the sidewalk, bouncing my ball, but that would never be enough to make him put on pants.

My dad sips coffee in his Italian suit. His shoes are Italian too. He says Italians make the best clothing and that any man who wants to earn respect in this world, who wants to tell the world who's in charge, shows that authority in his appearance.

"These left-wing liberals," he proclaims from behind his paper, "always giving away my money. My hard-earned dollar goes to fund these crack-smoking methamphetamine-using bums."

Every morning we hear about these abuses of his hard-earned dollar.

"Single mothers," he says. "They sit home in front of the TV with a house full of brats that don't go to school. The first of every month, the boyfriend shows up at the door to claim his share; then they use the rest to buy cigarettes, lottery tickets and junk food. And they populate the world with kids who'll grow up just like 'em, Deb. Always working the system. They could get jobs. But these liberal types perpetuate this vicious cycle by giving them hand-outs. I had nothing when I was growing up.

Look at me now."

He uses both hands to point himself out to us. He pauses. He picks up the paper and reads for one minute before launching in again.

"Where would I be if I sat around all day waiting for the first of the month?" he says from behind his paper.

He lowers it to look at my mom. She sips her coffee, doesn't eat until we're both out of the house.

"Foreigners! They can't make a living in Guatemala, so they come here to take jobs away from God-fearing Americans like you and me, Deb."

"Good morning."

"Morning, Consuela."

Our Guatemalan house-keeper walks through the front door.

On the radio, as a backdrop to my father's harangue, Sinatra croons, *I Did It My Way.*

Have I mentioned—I'm in love?

My love makes all this tolerable. Standing in the cold garage enumerating my grievances, my love overtakes the injustices. I think about her all the time—her silky dark hair, her glowing skin, her shyness, her gleaming smile directed at no one, everyone. I can't stop talking about her with my friends. They're sick of hearing about the new girl at school.

Some day I'll tell her.

"Look at this, Deb. Now they want to raise my taxes *and* tell me what I can and can't do. I can't smoke in a bar anymore, for God's sake."

"You don't smoke," my mother points out to him.

"That's not the point. The point is, the government says I *can't* smoke. They think they know what's best for me. I want to make my own choices. I don't want to follow their rules and regulations. I know what's best for me."

"We have to stop at red lights," I say, quietly to my

mother. "We drive on the right. Those are government regulations."

She beams me a wrinkled brow that I know means *don't press your luck.* But he can't hear me above his own words—and Frank.

At school today I try to keep quiet about the new girl. Her name is Beth. I write it on the first page of my spiral-bound notebook where others can't see it. I write it four-hundred thirty times. That's how many Beths it takes to cover the page completely. Her name is magic to me, although if I say it to myself enough times it becomes meaningless. I start to think about words in general, what they mean and how we assign a meaning to a sound. How we make these sounds to one another and how we can hurt people or please them by the sounds we make.

Jim snatches my notebook from me. He tears the Beth page out, wads it up and tosses it to Pete. They think this is hilarious. Pete opens it and reads before he throws it in the trash.

"Beth, oh Beth, oh, oh, oh, oh . . . ahhhhhhhh," Pete says as he makes jerking-off motions. Jim returns my notebook. Now I'll have to start all over again during German.

"Have you told her yet?" Jim asks, before adding, "I'm going to tell her."

"No. No please don't do that."

Pete and Jim smile at each other. They won't do that.

"I bet she'll put out if you play your cards right," Pete says, raising his eyebrows several times for emphasis.

I don't respond. They want me to think they've had sex but I don't believe them. I don't think they are any more worldly than I am.

"What you have to do," Pete says, "is get them hot. There's a special spot that you touch."

He's got our attention. Maybe he does know what

to do. But I don't want to think of Beth in that way. That's not important to my love.

"You have to touch them right here."

He puts his hand on his waist—to the side—just below his belt.

"There's a special place, just about there that does it. It gets them so hot that they can't stand it. They'll let you do anything after that. *Anything*."

"Where'd you hear about this?" Jim says.

"From somebody who ought to know," he says, wiggling his brows again.

Of course, I'm aware of the spot we all *want* to touch. That would surely do the trick, but you can't go around grabbing at *that*. Maybe there's something in what he says. Maybe that's how you sneak up on it.

I leave them in the hall and run to my German class. I'm already late. I grab the door to spin myself around the corner but my feet slip out from under me. I come crashing into the room on my butt. I get up, red-faced, my hand stinging from its slide across the door. Everybody giggles. Even Beth. I had thought about trying to talk to her after class but now I can't.

During our translation of Remarque's *All's Quiet on the Western Front*, I wonder just how you get to put your hand on that magic spot. You can't just walk up and casually start rubbing some girl there, can you? Wouldn't they want to know what the hell you thought you were doing? Wouldn't that be rude? Or would they really go into—like some kind of trance? Like when you rub a baby alligator's stomach and they go to sleep. When I really stop to think about it it's like they're a whole different species.

I could try it out with my friend, Nancy. I could pretend to be scratching my leg say, and my elbow might rub her there if I got in just the right position. Maybe she wouldn't notice anything unusual until suddenly, she got really hot.

In the cafeteria, Beth sits with some other girls. I don't know them. They're not popular. I'm not either really, except for being on the basketball team. Everybody knows who you are, at least. The girls I know are mostly second-tier. The first-tier girls all date starters. I'm just a sub. Last year I went out with Allison a couple times. She was a junior-varsity cheerleader, but she's moved up to varsity, so now she dates Chris, our starting center.

Nancy is second-tier. She's pretty, but we're both what Pete and Jim call *bookeaters*. We're more college-track than sports. Sometimes I think she likes me as more than just a friend. Maybe she'd let me try out the spot, as a sort of experiment. She's like—way into science.

Beth talks with the girls at her table but it's not big talk. Not like the first-tier girls who throw their heads back when they laugh and flip their hair. After Beth and her group finish eating, they sit for a while before taking their trays up. The first-tier girls hang around at their table until the first-tier boys come to sit with them.

First-tier girls never return their own trays.

At breakfast the next morning I try my love out on my mom.

"There's this girl, Beth," I say. "She's new. She's really pretty. I'm trying to get up the nerve to ask her to the prom."

"Well, that would be nice," she says. "But what about Nancy? I bet she'd go with you. I just think she's the nicest girl. You know, I hear she's been accepted to Princeton."

My dad's reading the paper. Not talking. I wish he would be himself, but while I have this conversation, he turns the radio down, muting Lorne Green's rendition of *Norwegian Wood*.

"Nancy and I are just friends," I say. "Besides she

Land of Many Uses   127

objects to the prom. Says it's part of a bourgeois ritual intended to transform women into what men think they should be. She says she'll be out on a camping trip while people like me, who buy into the dream, play-act at something they never should be, but will be."

"Communists!" my dad pipes up. I'm not sure what he has seen in the paper that evokes this reaction.

"What's Beth's last name?" my mom asks.

"Um . . .Estep"

My dad drops his paper.

"You're not slumming around with any Estep," he says. "That's final!"

I count them up. Nine words, directed at me personally—easily a month's worth in one sitting. I say nothing. The discussion is ended.

After school, I usually have practice, but Coach gives us the day off. I hang around watching for Beth at the bus pick-up area. I could get a ride with Pete. He drives a '91 Chevy Lumina that his dad turned over to him after an upgrade. "You comin'?" he asks. "Nah, I gotta do some work in the library."

I don't spot Beth until there's almost no one left. All the buses are gone. I summon everything that's in me. I'm going to talk to her. The prom's still a long way off. I have to work up to that. I should go for an ordinary date first.

She carries her books like girls do, clasped to her chest, further flattening what was already flat. I don't care if she's flat.

"Uh . . . Beth?"

She turns, obviously having no idea who I am.

"Hi."

"Hi."

"I'm Alan Sanders. I know you don't know me, but . . ."

This is going amazingly well. I'm not stammering

or anything.

"but I've seen you around school and I wanted to introduce myself."

She smiles shyly. Blushes.

"Did Casey put you up to this? I'm so embarrassed."

"No—Casey? Really, I don't know Casey."

Unless she means Casey Campbell, a girl in my homeroom.

"Anyway," I say. "I was wondering ..." now I'm beginning to panic. This is when it really gets hard. "I was wondering if ... you know ... if you don't have plans for Saturday night ... if you'd like to go to a ..."

She stops me cold.

"I ... I can't. I'm sorry. I ... I have to go somewhere with my mom. Listen. It was really nice to meet you ... but I ... I've got to go now."

She offers a delicate hand and we exchange something that is not quite a shake. Her skin is smooth and warm. Her grip is light but not mushy like some girls. I don't want to let go.

"Bye," she says, smiling. And she's gone before I can ask a question or raise an objection.

Over the next few days, the best I can do, is occasional eye-contact. Sometimes she smiles but quickly averts her gaze. I see the other girls at her table glance in my direction. I think they're giggling. I don't know whether they're laughing because they think I'm cute or because they think I'm such a geek. My armpits feel damp. Nervous sweat—the worst kind. Basketball sweat doesn't even smell that bad.

"What's the matter? Your new little honey not giving you the proper response?"

It's Nancy.

Could be, she's jealous 'cause I'm always going on and on about Beth. *And* she's seen the pages of my notebook. I've filled three now.

"Want me to put in a good word for you?"

"NO! No no no no no no. I'll work it out."

"You'd better get a move on. The prom's only 106 days away."

"What do you care? I thought that stuff was for the bourgeoisies."

"It is. I couldn't care less. I just hate to see my good friend go all limp and gooey over some little slut that won't give him the time of day, that's all. Listen, I have to go to the doctor tomorrow. Will you take me?"

"Well, yeah, sure. You OK?"

"Would I be going to the doctor if I was OK?"

"Well, I mean, you know, I hope it's nothing serious."

"Female trouble," she says flipping me a goodbye with her heavy braided ponytail as she walks off to her debate club meeting.

Why can't I just be interested in Nancy? I don't know any other girl who would talk to me about *female trouble*. I watch her mantis body disappear down the hallway with a boyish, bouncing step. Pete and Jim never even notice her. She is invisible to them. I wonder if they would see her if she had hips and breasts.

We don't have practice today so I wait for Beth after school, but again I don't see her until the last bus has gone. It occurs to me when I notice her slink out from behind a wall, that she has been sort of . . . hiding.

From me?

I follow at a safe distance as she walks away from the school grounds and into a nearby neighborhood where she slips behind a garage to emerge with a beat-up old bicycle. She tosses her daypack into its handlebar basket and rides off to the east.

***

"Why didn't you have your mom take you?" I ask Nancy. I'm driving her parents' car. She could drive but she wants me to.

"I want you to take me. I don't want to be alone and you're my best friend."

I don't say anything. I'm flattered, but she does have other friends ... girlfriends from the debate club and I've even seen her with a few guys. Could she be pregnant? There's that Rodney guy from the chess club I see her with sometimes, but I can't imagine her with that tub of lard. I shake my head, trying to clear that disgusting image.

The doctor's office is old, constructed of yellow, glazed brick. The chairs have been there for twenty years by the look of them. One wall is glass block, and through it, you can see the blurred shapes of passing traffic. As we wait, we leaf through magazines —*Better Homes and Gardens, Architectural Digest.* I search though the pile for *Dirt Rider*, or *Sky Diving* but the closest I can come is *Radio Control Modeler.* I tell her about Beth and the stashed bicycle but she offers no plausible explanation.

"Maybe she needs exercise."

A mean-looking nurse comes out and calls her name. The woman gives me an accusation of a look and I feel ashamed at what she must think I am guilty of. The injustice of it again.

I don't even smoke, drink, have sex or shoplift, Lady.

While I wait, I work on my Beth strategy. At the very least, I intend to get to the bottom of her mysterious bicycle behavior. When Nancy returns from her examination she apologizes for the length of time the whole thing has taken.

"That's OK," I say. I think she's been crying but she tries to hide her feelings. She buys me a Peanut Buster Parfait at the Dairy Queen.

***

"And they call that *art*," my dad grumbles into his paper. "My hard-earned tax dollar goes to pay some fruitcake to swing bags of human blood over a wine-sipping audience of perverts and queers."

On the radio, Jim Neighbors sings Don McLean's *Vincent*.

"He isn't still hanging around those Esteps is he?" He asks my mom. Although, if he lowered his paper, the question could be easily directed at its intended target.

I shake my head.

"No, dear," says my intercessor.

"Good."

I'm glad I've done something right.

I ride my bike to school and stash it near Beth's hiding place. I intend to follow her but I don't want the guys seeing me ride a bicycle to school like a seventh-grader.

My first task this morning is to quit the basketball team. I'm reluctant to tell Coach, but his half-hearted objection to my plan reconfirms my suspicion that my continued presence is not essential to the success of our squad. Now they will have more time to pursue my investigations.

After school Beth retrieves her bike and I trail along a half mile or so behind her. If I were to do this every day, I wouldn't lose any of the exercise benefits of basketball practice, as we ride for miles. The pavement gives way to a gravel road that's causes my skinny tires to wobble. The road enters the trees at the edge of the national forest. I've been here hiking or just goofing with Pete and Jim. A signs says "National Forest Campground, Bureau of Land Management." I lean my bike against a tree and follow on foot, darting from trunk to trunk like a guerrilla fighter in a war movie until I see her dismount. A woman, her mother I guess, stoops over a pot, which hangs on an iron hook above a fire. It's like a scene from some movie about medieval times. I watch from behind a tree as Beth kisses the woman and picks up a small child that runs to greet her. I can't make out the gender of the dirty child. The campsite is littered with household items and detritus of all sorts. My God! This is where she lives. The family seems to occupy two tents. From one of them, a pair of jeans-covered male legs and muddy-booted feet, protrudes from the dark interior. Old Milwaukee cans lie strewn about and two black trash bags bulge with protruding shapes similar to those of the cans on the ground.

The Esteps.

I imagine my dad's assessment of this scene as I creep away.

On my way home, I pass the reverse side of the national forest sign. *Land of Many Uses.*

I don't tell Nancy or Jim or Pete about my discovery. I watch Beth in German class. I almost can't believe that she looks so perfect, living the difficult life she must lead at home.

Home?

I think about our potential date. What would that be like? I borrow Mom's car, drive to the campground, chat with the mother at the picnic table while Beth touches up her make-up in the tent.

I find that I want to spend more time with Nancy—safe, normal Nancy. Nancy lives in a house. Nancy is going to Princeton in the Fall. She still hasn't told me about the doctor's visit. I watch her belly for telltale signs but I don't ask.

After school, I follow Beth again. I haven't completely given up the idea of her. I feel guilty for considering it. Am I turning into my father? I catch up with her where the pavement yields to gravel. I want to do something for her. I want to rescue her.

"Beth!" I pant.

She stops and turns. She doesn't seem all that surprised. We stand, straddling our bikes.

"Hi," she says.

"Hi. Listen, I ..."

"I know. You've been following me. I guess you've seen. Please don't tell anybody at school. I'd be so embarrassed."

"But why? Why do you live . . .here?"

"We don't have anywhere else to go. My mom ... she ... she's on welfare now. She had a job at the GM plant but when they moved the operation to Mexico she lost it. We had to move out of our apartment. We couldn't pay the rent and have enough left for food. We had camping gear and this was all we could think of. We're not the only ones. There are three other families here. On weekends, regular campers come. Every two weeks they make us up pack up and move to a new site. There's a two-week limit on each site. Now they say we have to leave because they close down the camp at the end of November."

"Where will you go?"

"I don't know. We might go south where it's warm all year. Florida maybe."

"That man. Is that your dad?"

"No. Cary's my ... my mom's boyfriend."

"Oh."

In my mind, I picture possibilities that I would rather not think about.

"And you ride your bike in every day. You look so . . .so . . ."

"Clean? The campground has showers. I try to look nice. It's hard when it rains but I always carry spare clothing in my pack, and I keep some clothes in my locker at school. Listen," she touches my arm. "I gotta go now."

She extends her hand before resuming the last leg

of her ride to her home in the woods where a mother, sister/brother, and some man wait for her return. Why can't the guy get a job? Why can't her mother get a job? I could get a job if I wanted. I think about following her back into the woods. I consider confronting the woman and man who would let the girl I love live like an animal. But I don't. I'm afraid of these people. And I'm ashamed. Suddenly, I want to be in my room with my stereo and my books and my model airplanes. I want to close my curtains on the world.

*

My dad's upset with me for quitting the team. Tells Mom that I'm a quitter. "The Sanders' are not quitters," he says. "Deb, if he's through with boyhood, it's time for manhood. I want him to go down to Groenigers. He can tell Charlie he's my boy—I sent him. Charlie'll find something for him. It's high time he starts finding out how the real world works."

The real world. Charlie Groeniger is my dad's insurance agent. Why am I taking German? *Guten Abend Herr Schmidt. Ich heisse Alan Sanders, ihre State Farm knabe.*

"Here," he says, directly to me—a week's worth.

He hands me a wooden hanger. From it, a new Italian suit, like one of his, is suspended. I put the jacket on over my T-shirt. It needs to be taken in here and there, but in the mirror I witness an amazing transformation.

My father stands behind me, actually smiling for a moment before he returns to the table to begin the day's first grumbling tirade. I feel the need to tug at my hair, adjusting it. I try on the pants. I turn to the side. I lean back. I pull them up before allowing them to drop casually onto my hips.

In this suit—I see the future. I see Yale, or at least Chapel Hill—drinks at the club, golf weekends in Arizona or Las Vegas. What I don't see anywhere in my reflection, is Beth Estep.

***

Nancy and I sit in her mom's car on a hill at the edge of town. She's drinking a Bud-Light and insists that I should as well. "You're not in training any more."

I sip at the liquid and cringe. Why does anyone like this stuff? The lights begin to flash, eerily strobing at the earth. You might think a space ship is about to descend but it's just the glide-path for the local airport. At last, the jet lowers itself over our car and lands out of sight, somewhere in front of us. I tell her about Beth as we wait for the next incoming flight.

"Should we do something? Tell somebody? I don't want to cause trouble for her, but I'm worried. Just think what that would be like."

"My mom knows this lady who's a social worker. I'll tell her if you want. I think that's probably the right thing to do. She'll never know you told."

I'm quiet, for a while, sipping my beer. "Nancy?"

"Yeah."

"When I took you to the doctor . . ."

She looks down, pensively.

"Are you . . . were you . . . you know, like pregnant?"

She smiles sadly. "I wish," she says. "I have a tumor."

I'm speechless.

"It's OK. Sort of. I mean, I'll live. It's not cancer."

"I'm glad," I say.

"Just who is it that you think I have been with, I wonder?"

"I don't know. I didn't really think that. I just didn't know what to think. I didn't want to pry."

"There's only one guy that I care about that much,

you know."

She pauses as the stobing starts up again.

"Anyway, do you know about the parts of the body? Like anatomy? You know, a woman's body?"

"Yeah, well pretty much."

"Well, there are these tubes, fallopian tubes they're called. And this thing I have has destroyed them. Both of them. They say it's very unusual. I don't have to have surgery. They're shrinking it with medication, but . . . I'll never have kids."

In the light of the next strobe, the streak of a tear is illuminated on her cheek.

"Alan?"

"Yeah?"

"Would you ... would you take me to the prom?"

For just an instant I give her a surprised look, but then I understand, she was never exactly what she pretended.

"Sure," I say. We lean toward each other and kiss. It's a platonic kiss at first. We are friends. We can count on each other. We kiss again, a little longer this time.

"Nancy?"

"Yeah?"

"Would you like to conduct a scientific experiment?"

She smiles. Then she laughs out loud.

"I bet you're talking about that story I told Pete," she says, taking my hand and placing it just below her waist on her left side. "Sure, let's give it a shot."

Arrowhead

She felt good about Tony for the first time in years.

He looked so peaceful there, slumped against the door.

What was that last thing he said? Something about guts. "You don't have the guts." Or was it, "You're a gutless bitch."

She walked into the kitchen to make another gin

and tonic, but found the ice tray empty. She never could get the proper timing for flipping that wire thing that turns it off and on. You flick it up and it produces so much ice that it spills out onto the floor every time you open the freezer door, or you forget to flip it back and the next time you look, the tray is empty except for the few food-particle-imbedded chips or the frozen, polluted leakage that lines the very bottom of the tray.

    She hacked away at the fragments for her drink. Should she worry about the yellow-brown color? Chicken blood? You could get salmonella—bird flu maybe. Of course, the alcohol might kill the bugs in the tainted ice if the cold hadn't already done the job. But viral diseases were more resistant to harsh conditions, oxygen deprivation, or cold or heat, weren't they? Hadn't she read that viruses could lay dormant on the moon or Mars if we accidentally dropped some there on our way to the outer planets or the Orrt cloud?

    She remembered to flip the lever this time and heard immediately, the sound of the already frozen cubes, falling into the tray—a satisfying sound. She searched under the counter for tonic. In the dim kitchen light, eight or nine bottles faded into the dark recesses of the cabinet. She pulled them out one by one, opening each to test the release of gas.

    Flat.

    She poured the dead liquids down the sink. On the fifth try she lucked out. The bottle sparkled to life when she twisted the plastic cap, quickly becoming too much of a good thing, erupting in a sticky volcano of effervescence, over the refrigerator, the floor, the cabinets, the countertop. She felt a bit too woozy at the moment to worry about cleaning it up thoroughly. Instead she wiped half-heartedly with a dishcloth that still lay nearby on the floor from the last time.

    The floor sucked at her sneakers. She frowned at it.

Dirty footprints were everywhere. Every time she went out to fetch the paper, she tracked dirt back over the tacky, sweet film until a layer of filth covered its adhesive coating. Now she would have to start all over again. She poured her drink from one of the big plastic gin bottles. They were so convenient now with that handle molded right in. She made a quick survey of her supply. Good. Four bottles left. When the tonic ran out she could switch to water or—straight gin.

    She took her drink back into the living room and sat back on the couch to look at Tony, trying to recapture the pleasant feeling she had before she had gone to refresh her drink. His head was tilted slightly to the left and slumped toward his chest. She tried to match the posture with her own head. She put her drink down and attempted to mimic his pose, arms at his side, hands open like Mantegna's *Dead Christ*. She smiled, thinking about how Tony used to say, "Who am I?" Then he'd lie back on the couch or the bed and hold his hands out like that.

    "Um, let's see," she'd say. "I know. You're the dead Christ." Then they'd laugh and he'd bring her a fresh drink. Sometimes she'd bring a drink down to him in his studio. He liked scotch—rocks with just a splash. Back in those days, Tony bought the best. Macallan eighteen year, single malt. The *nectar of the gods*, he called it. At the art exhibit openings he was always so witty and handsome, even if he never dressed like the people who came to buy his art. It was funny really, watching all those tuxedos and party dresses gather around his jeans and T-shirt. And hadn't *she* been a dish? She thought about her slinky black dress. A simple string of pearls was all the accessorization she needed. She watched as he fraternized with the society types, his biceps bulging from the rolled up sleeves of his T-shirt, a pack of Marlboros tucked into one. His eye would catch hers occasionally in a look that meant, *just wait till I get you home, babe.*

At home they always laughed about the Marlboros because Tony didn't smoke. Never smoked a cigarette in his life.

About five inches from one of his open Christ-palms, his tumbler of scotch lay on the floor—Usher's, a blend, not aged—six-fifty a pint. A single, unmelted cube remained in the glass. His arms no longer supported taut biceps. His thighs, once thick and powerful, with that definition of bulge and crease that athletes' legs or the legs of ballet dancers display, were thin now. You could easily imagine the bones underlying their loose shroud of flesh. That was funny too. Skinny arms and legs, but in between—a big, pregnant belly.

She would have to do something soon. She would have to move him, but not right now. She sipped at her drink until it was gone. She considered making another, but instead, she passed out.

When she awoke, she didn't immediately remember everything. Of course, she seldom remembered everything these days. It was a sound that had awakened her. A clapping metallic noise. Of course—the mail slot. Tony's head was just beneath it and now that she was awake, she saw the second onslaught of mail pour through. The first of it, what passed for real mail these days, bills—due and overdue—collection notices or threats of one kind or another, spilled across his belly and cascaded onto the floor. Next came the heavy stuff—glossy catalogs offering outdoorsy clothing, camping gear, garden tools, handmade furniture, modern home furnishings and all sorts of electronic goodies that she just might order one of these days. This heavy bombardment assaulted Tony's head, pushing it over a little further before the material slid thuddingly to the floor.

She shoved herself up unsteadily, wobbled her way over to the pile of mail, and selected one of the electronics catalogs. She carried it back to the couch and leafed

Arrowhead   141

through it, pausing first at flat TVs, then at treadmills. One of the work-out machines had a drink holder. That would be nice. She certainly could use some exercise. She used to be in decent shape. She thought again about her black dress.

She got up and went to the bedroom closet. The dress was still hanging in there, way back behind the loose frocks or sweat suits, which had become her daily fare. She held it up to herself. The full-length mirror showed lots of leftover body around the outer boundaries of the dress. She sighed and hung it back in its out-of-sight out-of-mind hiding place.

She made herself a sandwich and a new drink. After finishing her sandwich she decided that the time had come. She was going to have to move him. She bent over Tony and pulled with all her strength. He wouldn't budge. One side of his body came back off the door a bit but she realized that the other side was stuck. She could scarcely believe that she had done such a good job. She certainly didn't feel that she would ever have the strength to repeat her performance of a few hours earlier.

The feathered end of the second arrow protruded from her husband's chest. The business end of the first one—the stopper—Tony's big surprise—had gone all the way through his left arm and lodged itself firmly into their front door. She could maybe kick at him and break it off, but no. She remembered now, how he had demonstrated the strength of the shafts for her.

"Fiberglass," he had said. "Stronger than steel."

She was going to need a tool. She carried her drink down the steps to Tony's studio. The studio made her sad. He used to keep it so neat. Had a ritual of cleaning up after he finished each painting. There were his old paintings stacked against a back wall. Dust and cobwebs covered them.

"Back to back and face to face," he always told her

when she helped move them to a show or to his storage unit, back when they could afford that luxury. She pulled the first three back, looking at the images. She tried to remember the last time she saw these hanging in a public place. Ten years ago—maybe fifteen.

Why had she come down here?

Oh yes—the saw.

Tony's brushes were still in the bowl on his taboret. She tried to pick one up and the entire bowl came up with it. The solvents had long since evaporated, leaving the brush tips flattened to its bottom. But his tools were still in their orderly places on the peg-wall. A neat line-drawing surrounded each one. If a stranger took a tool down from this wall, he could easily relocate its proper place, even if he had no idea of its function or name. She selected a wooden handled saw with an eight-inch blade that tapered to a point.

She sloshed her drink on the way up the steps.

The room felt as cold as Tony's body. She had let the fire in the wood stove burn down. She went back down the steps, back through the studio to the woodpile under the deck. She carried up a few logs and got the fire going again. She sat on the floor in front of it, enjoying its warmth.

"There's nothing like the heat of a good wood fire," Tony always said.

Their stove was small, so small that you had to really struggle to get the wood in, but it was worth the effort. Even with the door closed it was better than a fireplace because you could still see the flames through the glass door and it gave off more heat. She dozed in front of it. When she woke up, it was roaring. She checked the magnetic thermometer on the stove-pipe. The fire was well into the *burn zone* where Tony always said it needed to be. She didn't know why exactly, but if that was where it was supposed to be, she figured that getting it even hotter might be better. She opened the door to see if she could force another piece in. She was greeted by a superheated blast that singed a few loose strands of her hair. She backed away, aware of the smell of burned hair. Some hot coals shot out at her, burning a hole in her sweat suit. A few more landed on the carpet. Using the electronics catalog, she pushed them back onto the tiles under the stove. She jammed another log into the opening and it caught immediately. She was unable to get it all the way in though. She tried to push it in with the door but it wouldn't close now. She decided to leave the door open until the log burned back. At that moment that she looked over and remembered Tony—with that arrow buried in his chest.

She felt bad about that but then she remembered the saw. She had a job to do. No time for sentimentality. When she reached behind him the tip of the tool made contact with the arrow shaft but she couldn't get enough leverage to make a proper sawing motion. She was so hot. She settled back on the couch and stared at Tony. The hunting bow was still leaning in the corner where she had left it.

She admired the bull's eye-arrow in his chest. She wondered if she could make such a perfect shot again. She thought about all the times she had watched Tony play darts down at the Watering Hole. Once he nailed two bulls then, with his third dart, he speared the feathers of one of the others. She had had a few drinks after all. She picked up the bow and four more arrows and stumbled back to the couch.

***

Stacy O'Connor drew the duty for the house-fire on the north side.

"It's a shame," the neighbor said. "They were quiet. Never bothered anybody. Sometimes I'd see her out in the yard, working in her garden. We didn't see him much, except when he went out for groceries and stuff. Always waved."

Stacy tried to interview the cops.

"The incident is still under investigation, Ma'am," the boyish officer said, making her feel older than her twenty-four years."

"Are you suggesting there may have been foul play?"

An older man, in a wrinkled suit stepped in to intercept any further grilling of the young cop.

"Foul play?" he said. He opened a pack of gum and offered her a stick, which she waved off. "You might say that," he said, grinning, chewing. "One of the bodies had six arrows in it."

Europa

Europa

Feed the cats. Walk the dog. Make the coffee. It's a job just to get your ass out of bed. Still, life's pretty good now that the kids are gone. 'Course I can't let on about how I feel about that to Elaine.

"Honey, you know Sandy and the twins? Well, I never wanted them and boy, am I glad they are finally outta here." Hell, she actually misses them.

When I say "outta here," I don't mean they're dead or anything—just gone.

If I admitted to her that I was glad, she'd be all over me to go for counseling again. She thinks I'm too insular—too self-absorbed. I don't need that shit. I don't need a shrink. Don't believe in it. That's for pussies like Gerald Forsenburg, my supervisor.

Like the other day ... he comes back to the office after his first "session" and "opens up" to me.

"God Paul," I feel so relieved to get that stuff off my chest. When I tell Joyce," —Joyce is the guy's shrink— "When I tell her my feelings, or about the secret desires I've been harboring, those problems seem to fall away and she absorbs them for me. It's sort of like going to confession, except she gives me meds too, and that really helps."

"Uh huh," I say, trying to suppress a giggle.

"Yeah. How bout you? You have anyone you can talk to? After my experience with Joyce I feel sort of empathetic. So if you ever need a shoulder, I'm here for you, guy."

Empathetic.

Pathetic's more like it.

"Thanks, Gerald. That's nice of you but I'm fine. Tell you what though, if you have any of those meds left over, like that pain medicine or anything I'd take it off your hands."

The guy just gives me a look and shakes his head.

Trying to shake off these images, I return to the bedroom with the paper and two coffee cups. Elaine's awake now. She stretches and reaches up to kiss me, a reward for my kind act. What a guy.

I try to concentrate on the sports section. But I re-read the same account of the free-agent draft for the third time. I keep thinking about Dave, from accounting. Dave's found religion. It's becoming a big problem because he wants to make sure everyone else finds it too. I can barely get out of the locker room for my afternoon run because I have to dodge Dave's sermons left and right.

Take yesterday. I'm lacing up my Nikes when he says, "Paul, I don't know whether you've allowed Jesus to come into your heart, but I want you to know that I have."

He always feels it necessary to stop dressing and look me in the eye while he harps on about Jesus. He gets way into my personal space, and no matter how I try to back away from him he presses in closer. He's carrying on about the Lord almighty, one leg propped up on the bench where I'm sitting, his balls swinging in front of my eyes, like he wants to hypnotize me with'em.

"That's great Dave, really. Did you see the Colts game yesterday?"

Jesus, if those balls get any closer . . .

"Paul, those worldly things no longer matter to me since I opened my heart to the Lord."

As he tells me about his heart opening, his legs open wider in front of me.

"I'd like you to come with me to one of our meetings and let Jesus in to your own heart. Without the salvation of our Lord Jesus Christ, I was heading down the road to ruin. It was the *devil drink*, Paul. It had me, excuse the expression, 'by the balls.'"

In order to further explain himself, as if I don't quite grasp his meaning, he grabs himself. In fact, he maybe grabs a little too hard because his already popping eyeballs seem to bulge out at me.

"I know you like to have a drink or two in the evening, Paul. But I've been down that road. I know where it leads. A man gets mean when he has a few too many. Just ask my ex."

He looks up sadly at the steam pipes, as though his ex lives up there now, in the locker room ceiling.

"Oh . . . I mean unless you already have your own

church. You're . . .you're not of the Jewish faith are you, Paul?"

"Look, Dave, I don't really want to talk about this. I'd like to go for my run and get back here and shower. I've got a 2:00 PM meeting."

"Oh sure," Dave says, palms up in a *no harm no foul* gesture. "I didn't mean to pry. Maybe you *are* Jewish and you just never mentioned it."

"I'm not Jewish, Dave." I decide to let the moment soak in for a second before I hit him with the truth. "I'm an atheist."

I can tell he's momentarily dumbstruck by this information. I finish tying my shoes and start for the door.

"Wait," Dave says.

It's pretty obvious that he has no pressing issues that are forcing *him* to get to the running track in a hurry.

"You mean you're an agnostic," he says.

"No, Dave, I'm an atheist. I don't believe in God. Gotta go now."

"Wait, I'll run with you."

"Great."

I look over at Elaine who seems content, examining the entertainment section. But I suspect she's not completely happy. She misses the kids. I can tell when they call, that's when she's truly happy. Her face lights up when she hears their voices. Maybe grandkids are what she needs. Maybe I don't have enough in my life either. That's what she always says anyway. She says I 'internalize,' I have enough. Enough house, enough car, enough truck, enough golf. But something is missing. I let out a sigh.

"What's wrong?" she asks.

"Nothing's wrong," I say.

"I suppose, as usual, that big sigh means nothing?"

"I told you, sighing is just a hobby of mine, like

having knee surgery."

"Right. I think what you really need *is* a hobby."

"I have golf and running."

"Yeah, and watching TV and drinking beer."

"Don't forget sighing."

"What I mean is …"

"I know what you mean. You want me to be like you. Take up painting and show flower pictures with all the little old ladies down at the art league."

"Something like that. Look."

She forces her section of the paper over my sports page and pokes at some kind of list. I see then that it's the special-interest course offerings at the community college.

"Photography," she says. "You bought that fancy new camera. What do you do with it?"

"I shoot photographs."

"Yeah? Where are they? I don't see them hanging anywhere."

I'm silent. I can't tell her that the last picture I took was a shot of my dick next to a tape measure. Sent it to my friend Jim in Indianapolis as a joke. She wouldn't think that's funny. She'd say it's lewd and childish. I wonder. Maybe she's got something. I guess Jim grew up. He didn't send me anything back.

"Sometimes we need a little push," she says, "to find our inner creative selves. That's what Daniel says."

I roll my eyes. Daniel is her painting instructor.

"Daniel takes it up the ass."

She slaps my arm.

"Well, I just think—that since you have this camera and lot's of time, you might as well use it. We could *both* show our work in the little old ladies' show at the art league."

We finish the paper and head off to our work lives with this idea hanging out there. She wants me to be happy. I want her to be happy. What does it mean to be happy?

Maybe I should pursue happiness. The constitution wants me to. Or is it the Declaration of Independence?

***

At noon, Dave's at it again. " So you don't believe in God."

"That's an affirmative."

"So where do we go when we die? You think we just disappear? What if you're wrong? What if you end up in Hell?"

"Well, that *would* be a shame. But I don't believe there is a Hell—or a Heaven."

I'm trying my best to lose him but there's no shaking the guy.

"Why don't you go on, Dave? This pace is too slow for you."

Dave is thin, fast—does a sub-38 minute 10K while I run 9:40 miles. But he lopes along effortlessly at my shoulder, his engine idling along at my pace. Maybe he can *save* me in the three miles we spend together. I'm not fat, but banged up in about every way you can think of, and the three beers a night that cling heavily to my mid-section, slow me down.

"How do you explain all this?" he asks with a sweep of his hand that takes in—I guess—everything.

I know perfectly well what he means but I say, "You mean the water-tower and the football stadium? I'd say second-rate architects and engineers are to blame."

"Boy, you are a hard case?" he says. "Listen, do you believe in the Ten Commandments?"

"Well," I say, "some of them are pretty good rules to live by. But when they order me to believe in a mystical being . . . "

I have to take in a little more air here in order to

continue. Dave is unaware that he has picked up the pace. To a certain extent I don't mind this, as his little push is probably good for me.

". . . a mystical being that lives in the sky and sees all and runs all our lives like some kind of celestial puppet show—I have to draw the line."

"What is it then?" he asks,

Oh boy, Here we go again.

"If you don't believe in God, if you're an . . . atheist," he practically chokes on the word, "then what keeps you from killing me?"

I knew this was coming. As ridiculous as that thought is, they all eventually ask me that. Am I some kind of real threat to these people? Do they think the only thing that stands in the way of my murderous acts, is a belief in an omnipotent being who at all times monitors me on their behalf, ready to stay my raised knife-hand?

"First of all, Dave, we have laws in this country, set down by our forefathers, making such acts illegal. I would be arrested, tried by a jury of my peers—maybe put to death for such a crime—even if it was only *you* I killed. Secondly, I believe that that would constitute an immoral act. I *do* know right from wrong."

"But how can you know what's right and what's wrong if you don't believe in God and our Savior, Jesus Christ?"

"You know what, Dave? Maybe you're right."

He smiles, seeing that his infallible logic has prevailed.

"Maybe I *should* kill you."

I decide then and there to enroll in the photography class. I am going to learn how to stalk, how to wait for exactly the right light, get the perfect composition, and capture the first image—of God.

If he exists—I'm taking his picture.

***

At the college I sit in a classroom with a few other geezers and geezettes and a handful of regular ball cap-wearing college types. The students have on their desks whatever cameras they own. The young ones finger cheap-looking little plastic boxes equipped with penile lenses that extend ridiculously at the push of a button. The old ladies caress sad cameras that their dead husbands must have used to take pictures of the kids— foolishly feeding the cute black bear cubs in the Smokies before the park service put an end to that practice. I know enough that I could advise them to throw these artifacts in the trash and head straight to Wal-Mart to get one of the penile plastic instruments if they have any hope of actually taking a picture. The old guys like me, with an eye for expensive technology, and more money than sense, fondle their bulky, fancy techno-cams with interchangeable lenses in special cases, ready for hot-swapping. If I, and those other two old guys, strapped our gear onto shoulder belts and donned our khaki bush uniforms and floppy hats we'd be as ready to rock and roll as Ansel Adams—if we just knew how to use the things.

Our instructor, Vicki, introduces herself and tells us what kind of photographer she is, explaining for us the differences between art photography, commercial photography and photojournalism.

Vicki is an artist.

While I should have my mind on the task at hand, I can't help wondering about Vicki. She looks like one of these lesbians. She's thin and angular with close-cropped hair. Sometimes I wonder if lesbianism is just a fad. I bet I could straighten one out. Elaine says you can tell if they're lesbians by the car they drive. Apparently, your lesbians favor Subarus. Maybe after class I'll follow her out and see what she gets in.

Europa

Now we each stand, introduce ourselves and tell why we are taking the course—what we want to be when we grow up. Turns out—not to my surprise—that every last one of us intends to make *art* with our little plastic boxes.

I'm especially interested in two of the young students. The girl, Asia, is beautiful and not as I might have expected from the name, ethnic. At least she's not ethnic in the same sense that I am not ethnic. She looks like she could be from Indiana or Ohio—short dishwater blonde hair, nice smile. Very clean looking.

It's been a while since I've been on a college campus. Asia, like almost all her compatriots, exhibits a deliciously exposed swath of flesh where her jeans and top do not quite come together. With some of them, I really would prefer that they did come together, but that's not the case here. A tantalizing parcel of tattoo peaks out from the waistband at the back of her jeans. That gap also reveals the two delightful little dimples that mark the uplands of every perfect feminine bottom. Finally, there is a glimpse of pink stretchy fabric that I can tell, is part of the thong that disappears into that heavenly space. I struggle against the urge to reach out and snap it.

Goddam!

And those eyes. Her dark eyes are big and soft, shielded by rather heavy eyebrows. Not quite Frieda Kahlo, but if there is any part of her that warrants the name she's been given, the eyes have it.

Then there's the young man, Lenndon, who is also beautiful, maybe more so than the girl. Lenndon is blonde—about 6'2," broad shoulders, extremely narrow hips. His blue eyes smolder behind little round wire rimmed glasses that I suspect he wears just for effect, since what I can see through them from where I sit behind him, is completely unrefracted. As a counter to this psuedo-intellectual façade, his intentionally-too-small T-shirt accentuates the over-development of his upper body musculature. He tops the whole ambience off with a head of well-unattended long curls, a look he has no doubt, been cultivating since the other envious mothers used to reach into his stroller to tweak his cute little cheekie-pies.

I notice that Asia, occasionally glances his way, her liquid eyes drinking in quick gulps of him before she's detected. She needn't worry. I watch Lenndon carefully. *His* eyes roam mostly over his own body. I catch him looking for reflective surfaces or watching his biceps as he discreetly flexes them for his own entertainment.

I want Asia.

This is silly. I'm over half a century old. She's what? 22, 23? Nevertheless, I now see Lenndon as my competition—my enemy. I cannot let him have that beautiful girl. I see what he is. What he is . . .is a vain asshole just like me.

At home I tell Elaine about the class and the people in it, minus a detail or two about my non-photographic ambitions. I describe the Subaru that Vicki drives. Elaine confirms that my instructor must indeed be gay.

At the next class, Vicki explains some basic principles of composition. We take notes about chemistry and water temperatures and we are given our first assignments. The following meeting finds us all stationed at enlargers and developing trays, watching for the first time the magical appearance of images on little pieces of paper under the red glow of the darkroom light. Whenever possible, I try to be in the darkroom at the same time as Asia. I brush against her accidentally in the close quarters. The others don't have much to say. They're not worried about anything but filling the world with more amateur photography. So I use my time to try to impress Asia with my vast array of useless, but interesting knowledge of the world, the universe, the Big Bang, music, sports, my theories on love—while I pretend to be absorbed in what I am doing. I try out my atheism on her to see if she is as stunned as poor old Dave. She's not phased. In fact she offers her own theories of the cosmos.

I find myself even more intrigued.

I ask about her name. "Why a continent?"

"My mother thought it was a pretty word. You don't?"

"Well sure," I say. "But Asia's big and you're pretty small."

"But at least it's a warm continent. Antarctica wouldn't have been very nice. Too cold."

"And the sound of it," I add. "I don't like its flow. And Asia's not all warm, you know. There is Siberia."

My main competition, the curly-headed Adonis, Lenndon, ceases to be much of a threat as he pursues a photographic avenue that allows him to be somewhere other than in class or the darkroom except on the occasion of critiques.

At the first crit, Vicki encourages us to be open with our comments. This is hard for the older crowd. Most of them have been trained to tiptoe around other people's feelings. I figure I'd better be nice too. So despite my total disinterest in Betty's flowers and Clarence's grandkids and Stan's landscapes, I give the best suggestions I can come up with; advice that, if heeded, could allow me to spend more than two seconds in front of these pictures.

We skirt carefully around Asia's images. Nudes. Faceless. We all suspect they are self-portraits but we don't ask that question. I see the other old guys stealing quick glances at her, trying to fit these pictures under that top and those shorts. But we speak only of light and shadow, exposure times, dodges and burns.

I think of Dodges too—like what I would like to do to her in the back seat of one.

Finally, after the polite dance around technique and process, it's my turn to be grilled. Why am I interested in pieces of rusted tin, old tools, paint peeling off signs attached to derelict motels along the old highway?

Asia wants to know.

I find that my tough-guy attitude becomes suddenly defensive when confronted by the slightest criticism. What's wrong with these people? Can't they see that my stuff is sophisticated, artsy—avant garde? I stumble and stutter a response. I feel my face flush. I've been caught empty-minded. I have taken pictures that mean nothing but look like "photography."

"I think what you are trying to tell us," Asia says, "with your motel photographs—is that something has been lost? Your youth maybe?"

She flashes me a look that contains the slightest hint of a smirk.

"What if," she suggests, "you were to contrast these pictures with the new Super 8 or the new Hampton Inn on the interstate? Maybe even . . . in a sort of double exposure, show us what goes on inside these motels. The old one should maybe show figures that look dated, like the women in Edward Hopper's paintings."

I nod, pretending that I know who Edward Hopper is and what his women look like. *I'm an assets planning manager for God's sake.*

"And the new ones," she goes on, "could show modern people."

"Or vice versa," I suggest. "I want to go back to Asia's pieces," I say, suddenly put off by the little know-all brat. "What is new about any of *this*?" I wave my hand across her nudes. "Why do we need more nude photos of cropped figures, curled up like *that* one with all the good parts conveniently hidden?

"And you would suggest what?" she says. "Wide open beavers?"

Betty pretends to be absorbed in her doodling. Clarence and Stan fiddle with empty film cartridges or zip and unzip lens cases.

Lenndon to pays no attention to this exchange. He's caught up in his reflection in the windows on the outer wall. He flexes his jaw muscles at himself and runs his hand over the smoothness of his bicep.

When we finally get to Lenndon's pictures, the ones we have *really* been avoiding because they are so blatantly dull, no one can think of a thing to say. But Vickie seems pleased with his insipid out-of-focus throw-aways. Am I missing something? Everything?

I go back into the darkroom to gather up my stuff. Asia comes in behind me but this time I have nothing to say. I just want to pack up and get the hell out of there. Suddenly, I feel a body press up against me from behind. The scent of her is almost more than I can bear. I feel the unmistakable crush of her breasts making twin dents in my sweater. Her arms encircle me, and one small hand travels past my belt and down into my pants. I turn back into her face, an action, which unfortunately has the effect of extracting her hand from its welcome location.

She smiles but seems suddenly shy—neither as tough as she was during the critique or as film-star sexy as she had tried to be just a moment before.

Did that really just happen?

"Are you free anytime on Sunday?" she asks. She seems to be trying to reinstate the confidence she had shown with my back turned. "Can you get away?"

"M . . m . . Maybe. I think so."

Why am I so nervous? Isn't this what I wanted?

"I've seen the way you look at me. Let's go on a shoot."

"A shoot?" I say.

"Yeah. You know, a film shoot." She smiles and comes close again. We kiss. "Meet me here at 2:00."

The revolving darkroom door squeaks and rattles, announcing Betty's entry. Asia and I pull away from each other quickly and busy ourselves with packing our gear—allowing our eyes to meet for just a moment as a confirmation of our Sunday date.

***

"So how was your critique?" Elaine asks. "Did they like your work?"

She's proud of me for taking her suggestion about signing up for the course and helping me figure out what the hell I should take pictures of. I sure couldn't bring those shots of my dick to the college.

"Um . . . yes and no. They thought it was well-done but lacked clarity of intent."

"Wow," she says, "That's pretty deep for an amateur photo group."

"Yeah but I think they're probably right. Look. Here's a picture I shot of the whole class."

I point out the middle figure. I've arranged the members of the class around a table, holding slices of pizza and soft drinks. They assume poses from the Lord's Supper.

"That's Vicki."

Elaine studies the photo—ignoring Vicki.

"*She's* pretty." She's points to the picture of Asia.

"Yeah, I guess so," I say. "Asia."

"Asia? That's her name?"

I nod.

"And this one's quite a hunk." She retrieves her magnifying glass from the drawer in her bedside table to examine Lenndon's golden curls.

"He's available I think. Um . . .I . . . I'm going on a shoot, on Sunday, with a couple of them."

"Oh yeah? Which ones?"

"Oh you know, a few of the old farts." I point to the images of Clarence and Stan.

"Want me to go along?"

"Oh no. You'd be bored." I say.

Europa

***

Asia and I climb into her rusted Datsun pickup and head out old Route 52. We stop at the first motel that I had shown in the critique and wander around the place. She jumps up onto the disintegrating concrete abutment that supports the dilapidated sign announcing the Belle-Aire Motel. She swings herself around, holding on to the signpost with one hand. I see the kid in her. She's stopped being tough now and tells me how impressed she has been with me and all my knowledge, and how I have so much more to offer than "boys" as she calls them, her own age.

So. I think, all that shit I shoveled actually worked.

We force open a rusty door. It smells. Homeless people have probably been living here. I photograph her nude. She poses in an old chair, looking sadly out the window. She says it's an Edward Hopper-like pose and I admit to her now that I don't know his work.

"Look it up," she says. "Let's checkout the new motel now—where the modern people go."

I get a room at the Hampton Inn. I photograph her again in this environment. At last we get down to the business we both knew we came here for and after some initial awkwardness on my part, it's every bit as good as I had imagined.

She drapes herself across my chest and falls asleep.

I must have dozed too. I look at my watch. Six o'clock. I'm getting nervous now, thinking about what lie I will try to pull off when I get home. Elaine has a great sense of smell. Is she going to notice Asia's scent on me? What are my "tells" when I try to lie?

I convince Asia that we've got to get out of here.

I admire her body as she dresses. Her shape, silhouetted against the light from the curtained window begins to arouse me again. She sees this and wags her finger at me.

"Naughty, naughty."

"I could be your father, you know."

"What?" she says, smiling, "You mean you fucked my mother?" She bounces back onto the bed to throw her arms around my neck and kiss me.

During the rest of the semester, we meet for *shoots* a few more times. I think about her when I can't be with her, but I can't risk everything for her. She knows that. She calls me at work. Gerald and Dave probably suspect something. When I'm on the phone to her, I'm all secrety and lovey-dovey, laughing and talking real low while I pretending to type on my keyboard. Dave approaches and I quickly delete the page of—*klkflkdjflkdjfldkjfdlskjflskdjfdskljfdslkjdklfjdlsk.*

I have had an affair or two in my time. Took 'em in stride. Just fun, no involvement, no phone calls, no notes stashed away in secret places, no hand-holding in public. A quick strike for both parties. One or two times at most. Smooth the skirt. Straighten the tie. A good time had by all. Maybe Elaine has even had an indiscretion or two. I deserve as much.

But this is different. It's more than the sex. I think about her all the time: at football games, at parties with friends that she doesn't know and will never know. Also, unreasonable and unhealthy jealousies begin to creep into my thoughts. What is she doing now? Who is she with?

This is no good.

I *want* her to be happy. I know she's not going to end up with me and she knows it too. Maybe this is just a diversion for her like I thought it would be for me. She'll dump me when she gets tired of all this attention.

The last time we were together, I almost didn't care about the sex. I explored her body with my hands and lips, kissing and feeling every inch of her, but not for my arousal really, or hers. It's like I just wanted to show her my appreciation. She's too good for sex. I have put her on some kind of pedestal—elevated her status to a kind of goddess. Maybe I'm sick. Maybe I *do* need a shrink.

I watch the clock, waiting for her daily call. When the phone rings I pounce on it with too much eagerness. Can she tell that I must sit staring at the device, waiting for it to speak up?

"I went to the dentist today," Asia tells me. "Had my teeth cleaned."

This is the kind of news a lover finds thrilling. I smile into the phone.

"He's about forty something, real cute."

I feel an adrenaline charge shoot through my arms like Novocain.

"He says, 'you sure have perfect teeth, young lady. Did you have braces when you were younger?'"

I feel myself slipping into the background—being supplanted by the advances, the accepted advances—of this *dentist*. I'm silent, thinking of the ways he could take advantage. Maybe he would drug her. While she's out cold he would perform his vile investigations.

"I gotta go," I say.

"Why? We just started talking. What's wrong? You can't be jealous! You're married. You can fuck Elaine whenever you feel like it."

"Did I ever tell you what a beautiful set of tits you have?" I say, spitefully. "Did you have tit braces when you were a kid? Gotta go."

What's wrong with me?

On Tuesday return to the college darkroom. The course is almost over. Final crit is next week. We get in whenever we can to work on our final projects. I don't care about that. I can hardly keep my mind on anything—let alone darkroom chemistry. I look for her but she's not here.

"Lenndon, hey."

"Hey man."

"Listen, have you seen Asia? She's got one of my lenses."

"Nah, I think she's out with some old guy she met—some dentist. I hear he's been . . . *examining* her," he says with a wink.

I want to hit him. How can he say that?

Examining her.

The thought of this loathsome examination makes me feel ill. I can't even respond. I stand with my fists clenched at my sides, my eyes closed, trying to recover from this abhorrent image. When I open my eyes again, Lenndon is smiling.

He knows.

On the way home in the car I try to put the image of the dentist out of my mind. But I can't. I force myself to see them together. I need the pain. She's performs acts with him that are meant for me only.
Nasty—horrible—wonderful acts. Where did she learn these things? He keeps his dental smock on. I wonder if it's white or is it one of those blue-green ones. I hope it's white. I can't take the thought of the blue-green one.

Elaine and I watch the evening news. After the weather and sports banter, they finish up with scenes of the heralded new young photographer at his opening downtown. His blonde curls bob up and down above the well-dressed artsy fartsies. Everybody is so fucking happy to look at this shit, wine glasses in hand. The camera zooms in on one or two of the stupid pictures that I know so well.

"Isn't that your friend Lenndon?" Elaine says.

"Yeah," I grumble.

Europa 163

The images are as totally wearisome here as they were in the critiques at the college. His whole point, it seems, is to take bad photographs. He told us this. In order to achieve this modest objective, he made sure that the subject matter was completely boring: the right rear bumper of a school bus, most of a candle, a paper plate, etc. He shot all these monotonous subjects with a cheap plastic throw-away camera from the Dollar store, always making sure to get so close that the pictures are completely out of focus.

"Brilliant."

That's the word I hear used several times as I try to shut my ears to the interview with some local-yokel arty type.

And on Lenndon's arm—is the lovely Asia.

"Oh look," Elaine says. "There's that pretty girl from your class too. You really ought to try to show *your* work. I think it's very good."

I feel suddenly ill. I go into the bath furthest from Elaine's chair at the TV and puke.

A couple weeks later, I'm going through my photos. I don't know what to do with them. They are really quite good. But Elaine has seen only the texture pieces. I can't show her my pictures of Asia in the motels, even though I had taken her suggestion to turn the double exposures into what may well be art. But then, in one of them I see something. It's probably my imagination. I get the magnifying glass out for a closer look.

In the double exposure I think I see a face spreading over all the outer windows of the old motel. Between the windows there is nothing.

I scan the photo into my computer and play around with the image digitally. I printout the results, cut the windows out and reassemble the enhanced images into a seamless collage, which I re-photograph. What I have now is a complete fraud. But what is art anyway?

In the windows of the motel the face of a lovely young woman with her head wrapped in a scarf fades in and out. Here and there, it is clear but it is blurred in some areas by a reflective, heavenly glow.

I enter the piece in the regional exhibition up in Indianapolis. The photo, to my amazement wins third prize. But more than that, it causes a huge stir. News photographers show up, interviewers ask questions. Where did I take the picture in which the Blessed Virgin appears?

It's evening now and Elaine and I drive out old Route 52 to the Belle Aire Motel where maybe a thousand people wait hopefully. Camper-vans, tents, folks selling souvenirs and concessions.

There's old Dave. Down on his knees like all the rest of them, waiting to rewitness the *miracle of Asia* as I call it.

"Well," Elaine says, "you said you were going to photograph God."

"Yeah, but as you can see, all I came up with was a fake Virgin Mary."

"Seems to be good enough for them," she says.

The next morning I awake to find my hands covering my private parts, shielding them I suppose, from some nocturnal harm.

Elaine's still sleeping soundly. She's welcome to the use of my body if she wants. She need only say the word, but she keeps right on sleeping. I cross my hands over my chest like a corpse in a casket. Grow up. Stop feeling so goddam sorry for yourself. I almost expect to find a continental shaped hole in my chest—a wound in the outline of my lover. I'm hoping that in time its topography will fill in again. Maybe a frozen lake will take its place, healing itself over like the billiard ball surface of Jupiter's moon, Europa.

C. and P. Charming

    Absently, she traced a finger through the puddle of spilled coffee on the tiled tabletop and sucked at her first cigarette of the morning. She could still look pretty at 55 if she took her time with makeup, but she had to admit, the dream had certainly faded. She walked to the bedroom and stood on her tiptoes to pull the box from the top shelf of her closet. She extracted the remaining glass slipper and tried to force it onto her left foot but it was no use. Poor circulation, or maybe it was just that time had taken its toll—smoking, not eating right, a few too many glasses of white wine—had caused her feet to swell. It all adds up. She put the box back up in the top of the closet and stood before the full-length mirror. She opened her dressing gown. Her breasts, although not bad, were no longer pert as they had been when they first met, all those years ago.

In the beginning it was all glamour...the castle...the parties...the elegant ladies and gentlemen...the royal visitors. And as sweet as she had always tried to be, she couldn't help letting a bit of smug self-satisfaction show through, especially in the infrequent presence of her stepmother and stepsisters. But they were all gone now and she had found it in her heart to forgive.

Drizella had always been the pretty one she had to admit, prettier even than she. Even after D put on a few pounds, the breast augmentation, liposuction and collagen had served her well. She was once again popular with the royals, so much so that she was at last invited to one of the balls whereupon she promptly suffered an aneurysm, or as C's hubby the Prince so indelicately put it, 'up and died.' Then of course there was that terrible business of the Heating and Air Conditioning Riots when Anastasia and Mum had been trampled to death.

"Jesus," she said to herself. That must have been fifteen years ago. Practically everybody has air conditioning now and never gives it a second thought.

They were childless and he had always blamed her. But sometimes she wondered. Her periods had been regular as clockwork. The problem could well be his drinking, which had become more and more of a problem after the first years of their marriage. Still, he had never treated her badly. At least he had not been physically abusive like some. She had heard the stories. Evil Prince Ficol of Theonia, the next fiefdom to the east, was notorious for his mistreatment of wives. But she had long ago concluded that in other significant ways, Prince C. was just the same as all the rest.

The Prince's drinking problem became so unbearable during the riots that she almost left him. But what would she do? Where could she go? Traditional schooling for women was frowned upon, if not strictly *verboten*. Yet she had educated herself during her lonely days and nights in the castle, reading everything she could get her hands on, from Kant to Kafka, but she had no marketable skills. And the more she learned, the more she realized that the Prince wasn't exactly the shiniest nugget in the pan. He had managed to make a go of it by surrounding himself with Daddy's cronies. Herbert, the bespectacled minister of defense and Konar the evil second in command, who actually pulled the strings, hissing all the time in the Prince's ear through his asymmetrical smirk, had worked for the former Prince.

Herbert didn't like her one little bit. He knew that she was smart. He talked down to everyone, explaining things carefully, spelling it out as though he were talking to a child. He even tried it with her but she could see in his eyes that he knew she wasn't buying. He was always afraid that she would be able to get through to the Prince and undermine his sinister plans, but he needn't have worried. The Prince would never have taken the advice of a woman on the affairs of state.

Sometimes she wondered why she had kept the second slipper. It served only as a reminder of everything the Prince had turned out not to be. She recalled the time she had grown so tired of being cooped up in the castle, luxury living or no, that she had put on a disguise and slipped out into the street for a cappuccino. She had been enjoying the sunny afternoon, seated at an outdoor table reading Kafka's *Amerika* when she overheard two young women talking about a man they had both apparently been seeing.

"Did he do you with the glass slipper thing too?"

"Oh, yeah! Worked like a *charm*," she giggled, "even though I knew all along it was plastic."

They both laughed.

"He never could really get it up though."

"I know," the second woman said with a laugh. "But I told him that it was OK. It happens to everyone."

"Yeah, me too. He must hear that a lot."

C couldn't even finish her cappuccino. She stumbled back to the castle, stopping only to throw up. When she got back, she pried open the locker in which the Prince kept the keys. She took a handful of them to the forbidden room adjacent to the dungeon. She began trying keys, under the barred gaze of a few prisoners who made *woo-woo* noises at her. She was still so angry and hurt that she was tempted to tell them to fuck off, but her gentle heart was way too kind for such language. She tried her best to ignore them. When the door creaked open, she found the room stacked to the ceiling with shoeboxes. She opened five or six of them and was not surprised at that point, to find transparent slippers in all sizes ... 5 tripple A's like her own, 6's, 7's 9D's and so on. She threw a 6 against the damp stone wall with every ounce of rage she felt, something she never would have dreamed of doing with her own slipper. It bounced. She picked it up and examined it. There was a small scratch in the crystalline surface where it had scraped the wall. She left the room without putting the boxes back in order or closing the door.

Upon returning to her room she had a good sob—one of those throwing herself face down on the bed, pillow hugging sort of things—expending most of her remaining energy for that day. She had just enough left when she finished, to take a candle to her right slipper and melt it into an ugly black clot.

You know how it is when plastic burns—smells to

high heaven—and the black smoke is laced with little filmy ribbons of carbon that settle on everything. When the drunken Prince smelled the conflagration he staggered his way up the steps to her tower room.

"What the shit's going on? You OK? Hey, you ... you melted your boot."

She threw the still-smoldering pustule at him. "Why don't you go down to the storeroom and bring me a matching one? I'm a 5 triple A, remember!"

But the Prince was silent. He didn't scold her about the keys and neither one of them ever brought the matter up again. Yet the issue hung in the stale castle air like a Plexiglas counterweight.

Still, there had been a silver lining to the incident. She knew he hadn't changed his philandering ways but he had shown her a new respect, sometimes even asking her advice on matters that seemed perplexing to him. The advice she gave him of course was almost always contrary to that which he received from Herbert and Konar. C was basically a pacifist and Herbert was always trigger-happy. Konar had been in the oil business before becoming the Prince's council and right hand man. Much of his advice therefore, was based on what would be good for his company. After all, he wouldn't be Chief Council forever. Someday he would return to the private sector.

In addition to the new light in which he regarded her, the Prince now took seriously her advice to go on the wagon. It was hard for him. He had the shakes and did a lot of sweating. Plus, in those days they didn't have AA meetings, so he pretty much had to suck it up. But in the end he felt better about himself and even cut down a bit on the womanizing and slipper distribution.

But alas, the uneasy truce in the Charming Castle did not translate into the fiefdom and the economy as a whole. There was general unrest among the workers as wages decreased and the economy sought out new lows.

"What we need," said Herbert to Konar, "is something to take their tiny minds off of the economic situation."

"That's right," added Konar, "and something to engage the enthusiasm of the Prince. What have you got in mind?"

"How's about a little war? The Theonians have had it in for us for years. But they're weak so we shouldn't have any trouble subduing them quickly. We'll tell the Prince we've detected a military build-up and we need to take the precaution preemptive measures. Besides, Their Prince Ficol is an evil man. We can always fall back on that."

"True, but what about all the other evil Princes. Some people might ask why we're just going after this one." (Konar)

"Eh ... fuck 'em." (Herbert)

"You're right." (Konar) "Besides, a war's never bad for the economy."

"Heh, heh, heh." (Herbert)

(Konar) "Ha ha ha ha ha ha ha ha ha ha ha ha ha ha ha ha ha ha ha ha ha aha ha ha ha ha ha ha ha ha ha ha ha ha ha ha ha ah ah ah ah ah ah ah ah ah ah ah ah ah ah ah ah ha ah ah ah ha ......"

"All right," Herbert said. "Enough already."

Konar had seen the evil laugh in movies and relished the chance to use it to good effect whenever the occasion arose. Inwardly he was glad Herbert had cut him short as he was overweight and the evil laugh put a strain on his enlarged heart.

***

"I don't know about this," C said to her husband when he told her of the war plans. "What real proof do you have of this threat?"

"Well, Herbert and Konar said that ..."

C. and P. Charming

"Oh, Herbert and Konar! If Konar told you to jump off the highest tower in the land armed only with your toothbrush you'd probably do it."

But she didn't press the issue. She could see that the poor man was nervous and indecisive. Instead she patted his arm and brought him a nice cup of tea, which he sipped as his darting eyes sought the comfort, which had formerly resided behind the door of the now empty liquor cabinet.

That evening as she lay in bed re-reading Carl Sagan's *Pale Blue Dot* for the third time, she heard scuttling noises and noticed mouse droppings on her bedside table. The Prince never came to bed until two or three in the morning, wandering around the castle in his bathrobe, drinking warm milk and watching re-runs of *Green Acres*.

She hadn't seen them for years. All three of them hopped up onto the bed, her old friends … Gus, Jaq and Perla. She had mixed feelings about this. She felt somewhat ashamed to admit to herself that they had always given her the creeps. In her years at the castle she had recurring nightmares about seeing them and screaming as they jumped into her open mouth and down her throat. And since they had been out of her life, things had seemed so—well—*clean*. She hadn't missed sweeping up mouse turds.

"Filthy creatures!" her step-mother Lady Tremain used to scold her, "I can't believe you hang around with those disgusting vermin. You know they carry diseases."

Their little outfits were exactly the same as she remembered..

"I can't believe you're all still … well … alive," she said.

They laughed in their high-pitched mousey way.

"We're the great great great great great great grandkids. I'm Gregor, this is Francois."

"Hey."

"And over here is Jennifer."

"Hi," squeaked Jennifer, dropping a little turd on the breadspread.

"But we know all about you. Passed down through the generations and all—you know. But listen. We came to warn you. Herbert and Konar are up to no good. That whole war thing ... it's a ruse. We were there. We heard it all. You've got to warn the Prince. He's making a big mistake."

C held up a hand to protest.

"Aw ... we know, the Prince can be a shit sometimes, but you know men."

The mice looked at each other and chuckled.

"But basically, he's not a bad guy."

The next morning over coffee, she told Prince C about her visitors and their advice.

"I don't know," the Prince said. Herbert and Konar ..."

She held up a hand to stop him, got up from the table and returned with a bottle of brandy that she had hidden away. She poured a small amount into his coffee cup.

"Here. Drink this. Just this once, and hear me out."

But in the end, the Prince was not strong enough for Herbert and Konar. When he confronted them, Herbert took the lead, explaining as though to a third grader, the sure-fire evidence of the threat the he and Konar had concocted.

After the Prince left them, Herbert said, "Something's got to be done about that woman."

"I'll work on it," said Konar with his patented smirk. He tapped his fingertips together with anticipation but stopped just short of evil laughter.

"One more thing," Herbert said. "Get somebody to put out some mousetraps. Heh heh heh."

"Ha!" laughed Konar. He couldn't resist. "Ha ha ha

C. and P. Charming

ha ha ha ha ha ha ha ha ha ha ha ha ha ha ha ha ha ha ha ha ha ..."

"Cut it!"

The next day Konar showed Herbert a pretty red box. Herbert opened it and smiled.

"That's good," he said. "I've seen this. Of course, you may be mixing metaphors."

Konar shrugged.

When C went looking for the Prince, to ascertain the outcome of his conversation with Herbert and Conar, she discovered him passed out on the couch in the main hall in front of the TV. A half-empty bottle of scotch sat on the coffee table. The glass lay overturned on his chest and his shirt was soaked through.

She felt tired.

When she returned to her room she found a beautiful red gift box on her nightstand. The vase was filled with fresh flowers. She opened the card and read 'from Herbert and Konar, enjoy.'

She remover the white satin ribbon from the box and opened it. A shiny red apple.

"Oh well," she said aloud.

***

She took the apple and a bottle of Fat Tire down to the forbidden room. She searched though the boxes until she found a complete pair of size 6's and put them on. She wiggled her toes. She sat down on the cold stone floor, took a pull from her beer and bit into the apple, which smelled ever so slightly of bitter almonds.

Singrad Advaard

The island was shaped like a comma. It was small, cold and rainy. The only village was situated at the pointed end of the peninsula about a mile from the airstrip. Wincross wasn't a scheduled stop. If everything went well you flew over it on your way to St. Lucies, where you could get a decent meal, a soft bed and spend a comfortable night before continuing on to the continent. But if there was engine trouble or bad weather ahead, you might be required to hunker down on this miserable outpost a thousand miles from Labrador, a thousand miles from St. Lucies and two thousand miles from the coast. It was engine trouble that had forced me down on this occasion.

Ivar, the island's only mechanic, had been kind enough to allow me to stay in his home. He was a nervous man who seemed overly concerned with my comfort. Was I warm enough, was the bed firm enough, did I need more tea or perhaps a beer? He watched me for any signs of discomfort and stood wringing his hands until I said good night. Unfortunately, shortly after I went to bed he suffered a heart attack. During the days that followed Ivar's death, a shaggy collection of people—who, most said, were Ivar's disreputable distant cousins from some far-off island—descended upon the house, seizing the opportunity they had apparently been waiting for, to move, along with their attendant chickens, goats and milk cow, into Ivar's house. Naturally I felt compelled, after offering my condolences, to leave the squatters to their new home.

I had enough money for two or three nights stay in a room above the tavern, during which time I made the acquaintance of a local by the name of Singrad, who claimed that he could fix my engine, without aid of schematics or original equipment parts. Furthermore, he would only take on the job, he told me, if it entailed what he called 'a challenge.' He had no interest in simply plugging the correct pegs into the correct holes. He intended to manufacture any necessary parts himself. They would, he assured me, be superior to the originals.

I had little choice but to trust him, although from the look of the non-ambulatory farm equipment and small household appliances scattered over his weed-infested property, he had not been all that successful in getting far less lethal devices up and running.

"When can you get started?" I asked.

"After a time," he said, taking a leisurely bite from

his sandwich. "You people from the *world*, you're always in such a hurry. Here on Wincross we go by island time. But as you can see I have many other jobs ahead of me before I can tend to your flying machine."

I took a look around. I could see nothing other than the pile of junk out in the yard. If I had to wait until all these objects began to move under their own power, I would be in for a long stay ... but I had no choice.

During the day I had little to do other than wander around the island on foot, so I followed the peninsula to the head of the comma where I made my way inland, away from squawking gulls, crashing waves and nesting puffins. On a treeless outcropping at the edge of a tidal pool, in the, rocky, rain-swept interior, I came across a disintegrating old cabin, well on its way to a merger with the landscape. My most pressing need at the moment was to find less expensive shelter than the room I was currently renting, as I was quickly running out of money. Even in the poor condition in which I found it, the shack presented an opportunity to put a free roof over my head for a few days. Inside, I was able to coax a smoky fire from the woodstove. In one corner, the rotting roof had collapsed, allowing the sky to pour in. I had spent three days on the island and in that time there had been about five rainless hours. This was not one of them. After warming myself sufficiently I zipped my waterproof windbreaker and made the long trudge back to the village.

In town, I used most of my remaining money to purchase groceries and a few items to hold me over until Singrad's repair was complete. Passing the airstrip I retrieved the two books I had brought with me from the plane, before making my way back to my new home.

I was able to cook a simple meal on the stove, which also served as my source of heat. Afterward, I tried without success to read by the light of the fire from its open door, before bedding down for the night on the floor.

Singrad Advaard

I used some old burlap bags for a mattress and an Army blanket from the plane for cover. During the night, the rain stopped its kidding around and came down in torrents.

I was awakened by its seriousness creeping into my sleep. I reestablished my bed on the table, which listed to one side on a damaged leg. The table was not long enough, of course, to accommodate my body in anything other than a fetal position so I spent a most uncomfortable night of shifting here and there until the first faint hint of another dismal morning broke over the horizon. When the light was sufficient to illuminate the grim interior, I found the floor covered with about an inch of black water.

I shivered there over a cup of coffee for as long as I could stand it, bracing for the sodden walk back into town to see if I could prod Singrad into getting busy with my repair. As I gazed out through the fog and drizzle, I thought back to other mornings, before Kendra left, when we had been more than happy to silently share mugs of coffee at the edge of a fire ring, tent-camping in the Upper Peninsula ... or along the peaceful shore of some alpine lake. After those happier days came to an end, I had tried to convince myself that I could be content with my own company, flying from outpost to outpost, getting odd jobs here and there that allowed me to buy enough supplies and fuel to move on to the next location ... seeing the world from a perspective available to so few. Even before Kendra got sick of waiting for me to *'get some kind of life'* as she had so often put it, I had come to the conclusion that no matter what our situation, deep inside, we live out our lives alone. Now, here I am—alone, wet and cold. But even if she were here, would I be any less alone?

When I arrived at Singrad's place it was still only 7:30 and I could see no light inside. It was too early to go banging at his door so I huddled under the roof of his front porch until I heard stirring inside. When I felt that it would be appropriate to make my presence known, I knocked.

The woman who answered the door seemed far too young and attractive for the grizzled old mechanic, nevertheless I tested the notion of who she might be.

"Mrs. Eh ... Mrs, Singrad?" I didn't know Singrad's last name.

"Oh no, sir. I'm his secretary."

"Oh. Oh ... yes ...I see. Well, is he available? I'm sorry, you see, about the early hour, but I need to talk to him, to find out if he could possibly push my repair to the top of his list."

"Did you have an appointment?"

"An appointment? Uh ...no...but I did talk to him about my airplane."

"Oh, yes. I think he did mention that, sir. Which airplane was yours then, the blue one?"

"Um ... no in fact. It's red."

"Oh, I see. Could you excuse me for a minute sir?"

As she turned to walk away, the rising sun passing through an interior window, penetrated her thin nightgown, revealing a shape that made me temporarily ache for the comfort of a woman.

She closed the door behind her. I could not help wondering why Singrad's secretary was dressed in such intimate attire in his home. What would she be doing there at such an early hour. Was there a Mrs. Singrad inside? Was this secretary available, or if I approached her with some of the thoughts I tried now to suppress, would Singrad object? She was after all, only his employee—his secretary—a title that implied less than appearances seemed to indicate.

As I waited, I tried to remember any other aircraft that I had seen on the island. I could recall none. Mine was the only plane parked at the airstrip, lashed down against the constant windblown rain. I stood for what seemed like twenty minutes until she returned with a clipboard.

Well I'm afraid sir, that Mr. Singrad will not be able to get to your problem until he has seen to the blue plane, the white plane and of course, the toaster-oven. Could you come back, say, next Wednesday? I'll put you down for 3:30."

I craned for a glimpse behind her, of the busy Singrad, but she kept shifting her position in the doorway, intentionally blocking my view. I thanked her and resumed my walk back into town. I wandered about asking shopkeepers about Singrad's reputation for promptness and quality of work.

"Oh, sir," I was told by one, "unfortunately, I would have suggested Ivar, but sadly he passed away only a few nights ago. He was a wonderful mechanic sir, but he was always such a loner, and we heard that some evenings ago he had a house-guest. Most unusual. His relatives, who are now staying in his home, concluded that the stress must have been too much for him. But Mr. Singrad Advaard, sir, is as fine a repairman as you will find in these islands, now that Ivar is gone. In fact, I have entrusted him with the repair of my toaster-oven."

I gave the man a puzzled look.

"These islands? I thought this was the only one until St Lucies."

"Well, just to the west, about thirty miles from here, there is Port Waltrude. It's much smaller of course but they also have a mechanic. But Singrad sir, is as I have said, the finest in these islands—now that Ivar has gone to his rest. Be assured sir, you could not have crash-landed in a more fortuitous place."

Upon my return to the cabin, I found smoke rising from the chimney. Cautiously I pushed open the door and was greeted by the aroma of delicious cooking smells. A smiling man greeted me. He was bearded and dressed in some rustic outfit comprised of animal skins. He looked like some kind of 19th century French-Canadian trapper.

"Um ... hello," I said. "I'm sorry to intrude. Is this your cabin?"

"My cabin? Oh no. I thought it was yours," he said with a laugh, in the accent of a 19th century French-Canadian trapper. "I am Broussard. I am, as you, stranded on this godforsaken backwater of a hellish rain-soaked-shit-hole."

"You ...you know who I am?"

"Everyone knows. You are the asshole owner of the red aeroplane who caused the death of the mechanic, Ivar. And you are the reason we wait in a long line behind white aeroplanes and toaster-ovens for a way out of this miserable tundra. I am the owner of the blue aircraft. But join me in some wine and *gigot en chevreuil* and we will become drunker and wetter together."

Over the course of the long evening, we drank and shared stories of travel and misadventure as viscous raindrops battered the roof and windows of the leaky cabin. It seems that Broussard's craft had suffered structural damage to the stabilizer when he got caught up in turbulence from a 747 that he thought was well out of range. When I yawned for the third or fourth time and glanced at my watch, it was 1:34 AM.

"I think I'm ready to hit the sack," I said to Broussard who was obviously wide-awake.

"The sack?"

"Sorry. It's an expression. Bed. I need to get some sleep."

"Oh yes, of course. You must take the table. I will sleep on that shelf."

Just then a knock at the door, startled both of us.

"I say," said the intruder, poking his head in the door. "It's a frightfully nasty night out and I was wondering if you chaps would mind if I joined you at the fire? I'm soaked through to the bone." Cheerfully, the newcomer bounced into the room, removing his cap and extending a hand. "Perkins, Jerome Perkins. I'm the owner of the white aeroplane."

I made an effort to stay up with Perkins and Broussard as long as I could hold out. Broussard and I had managed to plug enough of the leaks so that the floor no longer held standing water. Perkins, who had been staying in a cave in the interior hills had seen our light and smelled our fire. He told us that the sight was so downright cheerful that he had decided to see if he could join us, just for the evening. It seemed that he had been on the island for two or three months, waiting for his repair. Ivar had been too busy to take him on and had passed the work on to Singrad. Ivar, just prior to his untimely death, had been thinking of moving to Florida and was hoping that Singrad could gradually take over all of the island's repair work. I remembered then, the posters of Disney World, plastered over the walls of Ivar's house.

When I asked Broussard and Perkins where their airplanes were, they explained to me that before any repair could begin, they had been moved to the hangar. When I commented that I had seen no hangar, they told me they would show me on the following day. We managed to clear away a relatively dry area of floor near the stove, where Perkins slept. Broussard took to his shelf and I to my table.

The next morning after Broussard prepared a delicious breakfast of puffin eggs and fried cod strips, we hiked through the rain, fog and gloom to a rocky ledge near the landing strip. Built up against its opposite side was an immense wooden lean-to, covered by a leaky tin roof. Sheltered inside were Perkins white plane and Broussard's blue plane, a crude sailing vessel and what appeared to be a missile that was being repaired in stages. A jet or rocket engine, sat next to the tube-like craft, having been unbolted from its housing near the tail assembly. Various tools were scattered about the disassembled engine and on a workbench adjacent to this craft, sat the toaster-oven—the troublesome device that seemed to be at the heart of the hold-up.

I picked up a set of drawings from the bench. They were rendered in the hand of an unskilled draftsman, probably Singrad himself, and appeared to be attempts to visualize the possible shortcomings of the appliance. I could see that he was going at it all wrong. The heating element in one of the drawings, was attached to some kind of clock. In another, a fan was shown, with arrows indicating wind direction, blowing out from its blades toward some kind of deflecting screen, apparently for the purpose of dissipating heat produced by the clock, from which wavy lines indicative of radiation emanated. I turned the toaster-oven in my hands. On the front of its case there was an on-off switch. Behind the switch, I discovered a broken wire. Using my pocketknife, I stripped the two ends of the wire, and spliced them together as Perkins and Broussard watched with inexplicable interest. I plugged the oven into the wall socket and flipped the switch. Heat immediately began to radiate from the now repaired appliance.

"This is ridiculous!" I said.

"Good show, old man," Perkins said, "I say. You've made short work of that major obstacle."

"A child could have fixed it!" I protested. "This genius, Singrad needs to draw up a set of plans for this?"

That night, over dinner, Perkins, Broussard and I discussed our options.

"We must go to him and demand immediate action," I said.

Even as I made this suggestion I was second-guessing myself. I did not know enough on my own, to repair the engine, but at the same time—putting my life in the hands of this mechanic who had such difficulty in finding and repairing a simple broken wire—I did find somewhat troubling.

"Impossible," Perkins said. "You'll never get past that secretary of his."

"Ooo la la," said Broussard, with a shake of his hand and snapping of loose knuckles. "That one is a most tasty dish."

Perkins raised his eyebrows twice in agreement.

"Why are you in such a hurry, old man?" Perkins asked. "It's rather pleasant here. No pressures. Winter is coming on, but we could fix this place up."

"I saw some cans of paint at Singrad's hangar and there are brushes in the tool shed out back," Broussard added.

"Here's what we'll do! We'll start making repairs tomorrow. We must keep active and productive through the long nights. We mustn't let ourselves go. I've seen what can happen to men, living in isolated conditions in these latitudes. When the dark settles in for months, it takes its toll on the soul. It starts simply enough—arguments over who'll gather firewood, who'll do the cooking, which one will go for water—and before you know it, you're at each other's throats. I'll begin straight away, building a running track. We'll jog three miles a day, and in the evenings we can do readings. You can start tonight, old man," he said to me. "I took a look at the books you brought in. They look quite interesting. You read a chapter of yours and I'll read one of mine."

"I play the guitar," Broussard offered. "We can sing songs of our homelands. We'll get to know each other well by winter's end."

They seemed positively delighted at the prospect of spending the winter in this nightmare of ineptitude and squalor.

"You have a guitar here?" Perkins asked Broussard.

"No, but with some materials from Singrad's shop and whatever I can find in this place, I will build one."

"That's jolly well, old man," Perkins said, clapping Broussard on the back. And I always thought you French were a lazy lot."

"French-Canadian," Broussard corrected him.

I could see that I would get nowhere trying to reason with these two. The following morning after breakfast, I hiked alone to the hangar. Still no Singrad. I picked up the repaired toaster-oven and headed off to his house where I was once more met at the door by the nightgowned secretary.

"Did you have an appointment?"

"No, but I need to talk to him about my airplane."

"And which craft was that, sir, the blue one?"

"No! I'm the red one. Look …" I tried to calm myself. "I have to get out of here before winter closes in."

"Oh yes sir. Winter in these islands can be very harsh. I hope you have set in a store of supplies and wood. Many of our previous customers have found that a running track of some sort can be helpful, not only in relieving the monotony but also it is said to help the circulation in this damp."

"I don't give a damn about my circulation!"

I regretted my outburst, which had caused her to give me a rather shocked look. I made every effort to control myself.

"I want to get my plane repaired and get out of here. I promise you that I will get my exercise somewhere else. I'll keep up proper circulation in some civilized place."

I felt bad once again, having implied that the poor woman's home island was something other than civilization.

"I'm sorry sir, but he has promised the owner of the toaster-oven that it will be repaired soon. As you can see, even now he is hard at work on drawings which will lead to its restoration."

With that she opened the door a bit and stood aside so that I could see Singrad at a drafting table, busy with a drawing, occasionally looking up at the ceiling and scratching his head with the eraser end of his pencil. Clearly, he was devoting all his concentration to the problem.

I tucked the oven under my arm and walked into town to see the shopkeeper-owner of the appliance. The man was elated.

"Oh sir, thank you!"

He plugged the oven in and made toasted cheese sandwiches for each of us.

"I tell you sir, that Singrad ... what a genius! And only two months this time. With these dark winter nights coming on, it can be so difficult without a properly working toaster-oven. And it's good that he has hired someone to make his deliveries for him. With that worry off his mind, I expect that he will become even more efficient. What do I owe him?"

*

When I arrived back at the cabin I found Perkins and Broussard, busily cleaning and cooking. The windows were hung with curtains made of some flower-patterned material. The table was set for five. Candles and an arrangement of native lichens and mosses served as a centerpiece.

"We have invited Singrad and his secretary to join us for dinner," Broussard explained.

*

While the secretary and Broussard made eyes at one another, Perkins and I made small talk with old Singrad as a lead-in to my request for more timely repair work.

"The missile we found on your workbench, what's the story on that?" I asked.

"Story? Oh, it's nothing really. We found it washed up on shore and several of us thought that if we could get it to work, it would be a welcome addition to the island's Department of Defense."

The Department of Defense turned out to be Singrad, the shopkeeper I had met previously and Ivar before he had sadly passed. Prior to the missile, their arsenal consisted of a couple rifles and a harpoon gun.

"But the problem of the toaster-oven has been solved at last," Singrad said. "It has mysteriously vanished. Therefore I am free to move on to the next task. And since you," he waved his hand graciously to include Broussard, Perkins and me, "have been so kind to me and my dear secretary, Gertrude." Here he paused to indicate Perkins. "Your name, sir, will advance up the list."

"Oh that's quite all right old chap," Perkins said, as I fumed. "I'm perfectly content to spend the winter here. And I'm sure my colleague Broussard will be quite happy as well over the coming winter."

Perkins winked at Singrad and me.

"Oh yes," I said, first nodding my thanks to Perkins for his deference. "And I almost forgot. I have something for you, Mr. Advaard."

"Please, by all means call me Singrad."

"Singrad," I said, smiling.

I produced the money the shopkeeper and I had agreed upon for the repair of the toaster-oven and handed it over to Singrad who seemed not in the least surprised that the repair had been made and delivered for him.

"Are you quite sure," he asked me, "that you wish to leave? I could really use someone of your expertise in the repair of small appliances."

The next day, Broussard, Perkins, Singrad and I towed my craft to the repair hangar. I must admit that I was surprised at the skill the old mechanic displayed in working on my engine. He began by looking the engine over and drafting some plans, which allowed him to disassemble it, locate the problem, a broken piston ring, and reassemble it once again. In a matter of two days, the motor was humming like new. There was a delay of a few days more for the weather to improve to conditions of lighter rain and lighter fog, before I felt that it was safe to resume my journey. I shook hands with my cabin mates, and hugged old Singrad. Broussard and the old man's secretary, Gertrude stood with arms encircling one another, waving goodbye, as I took to the air once more. As I gained altitude, I circled the comma shaped island once before heading east. I had not gone more than twenty miles before the engine began to sputter. Below me and to the west I could make out white rollers crashing against the rocks of a question-mark-shaped island, even smaller than Wincross. This must be Port Waltrude that the shopkeeper had told me about. I was afraid to turn back to Wincross and even more afraid to attempt going on to St Lucies which lay still so far ahead. I had no choice but to put down. The small airstrip was easy to pick out. The attendant, bowing into a stiff wind, came out to meet me holding his blowing rain-hood down with one hand and clasped his collar closed with the other. He helped me lash down my plane and guided me into the little hut where he poured me a fresh cup of coffee.

"Engine trouble?"

"Yes," I said, defeated. "But I'm told you have a good mechanic here."

"Oh yes sir. One of the best. Gringaard is his name—Gringaard Advaard.

He's the brother of the mechanic on the island just to the west. Perhaps you noticed it as you passed over. But I don't know when he'll be able to see you. He's extremely busy just now, with winter coming on. I'm afraid you'll have to make an appointment with his secretary."

Light drops of rain changed into fat splatters. A few wet snowflakes joined into the mix as darkness descended over the little hut.

Mr. Friendly

Mr. Friendly

Amanda is dead.
That's the news I receive in Terry's email. The last time I saw Terry was Christmas, four maybe five years ago when we went back to see the few remaining relatives and friends in my hometown. Ellen had never met him or Barry, my two closest friends from high school. We get

cards at Christmas from Barry. Terry emails me now and then.

Me? I'm no good.

That's what I tell everyone. It's my excuse for actually *being* no good. I never send cards. I never initiate emails. I respond to them—sometimes. Or I just look at the name and the subject line and don't open them. I feel too guilty to delete them unopened so they sometimes sit there in my in-box, unread in bold type. The business messages all around them come and go. I have no great fear of business.

Here' an old message from David. (daaaa-veeed) Daaveed ees from Colombia. We were good friends once. He used to say, "Char-less," he couldn't say Charles. "Char-less, jew are my good friend. Someday we weel go to the Amoson Reever where I grew up. We weel drink many bottles off wine on thees reever and we weel fock some girls."
The subject of his message is *Avatars Test*. I have no idea what that means. It's been languishing in my inbox for a month.

Here's another one from an old girlfriend. *A blast from the past* is its claim. It's been there for two years. It was only two years before I got it that I even discovered email. I wonder sometimes, what's in that message? I should open it. Maybe she's dumped her current boyfriend or husband and wants to rekindle the old flame. Wanted to, I should say. Surely she's concluded by now that her electronic probe never landed safely. She probably never imagined that it's in my inbox untouched, like a Mars-lander whose come-to-life signal is never sent. These messages never erode or rot. If the world ends they will still be floating out there until the last bits of energy in the universe wink out completely.

I stand to stretch my arms. When I look over the carpeted walls of my cubicle I can see into all the other

Mr. Friendly

cubicles. There's Doris. She's with a client—two clients actually: a father or husband or boyfriend and his wife or girlfriend or daughter, or possibly his daughter *and* his girlfriend. I think the female is younger than the male but it's really hard to tell with fat people. Doris is trying to explain to them why his or her disability check has been discontinued. I'm trying to look busy so I won't have to meet with my clients. When I looked out the peephole into the waiting room I saw them, a fat woman and her fat child. The child is probably female—although I couldn't quite tell from the tiny fish-eye image. They're waiting for their number to pop up.

    I try to will the hands of the clock around to five. They can take the bus back down here and try again tomorrow.

    Why do they call it a cubicle? Shouldn't a cubicle have a top? A cube has six sides. This thing only has five. I guess if it had a top though, it would be a cube. Dave's not in his cubicle. Sandy has a client with her. Stephanie has two. She sees me and raises her eyebrows.

    Sandy stands to dismiss her case, offering her hand, which the woman does not acknowledge. Maybe she doesn't understand or it could be she's not feeling friendly after her case is denied. Regardless, this is bad news for me. I hear the ping that means *next*. That's me. I sit back down at my desk as I hear the door open. Sandy shows my clients in.

    "Mrs. Hobson, this is Mr. Friendly."

    "Hello," I say, offering my hand to the obese woman. "Charles Friendly. Won't you have a seat?"

    The child, it turns out, is a boy. I think. It's probably a teenager, thirteen or fourteen. It wears boy's clothing. Its face is chubby and girlish and its hair is long, so I'm still not quite sure. My safest course is to try to ignore the child.

    "So, Mrs. Hobson," I say as I look over the paperwork, "you haven't worked for three months."

"That's right. I can't work because of my diagnosis—bi-polar."

"I see. And you are seeing a doctor regularly?"

'Well, I did but I ain't been for a while."

"And you have medication?"

"Well, I had it— but it run out —before they let me out."

"Out of?"

"I was in county," she says without making eye-contact.

"I see." I look over her chart and see that she was in the county jail from April until October. Bad checks.

I go through the usual explanations about reinstatement of her SSI only after she has seen Stan, our psychiatrist. She doesn't want to do that of course, because it's a lot of trouble—phone calls, three weeks to get an appointment, bus 18 transfer to bus 23 to bus 8 then the same circuitous route back to her trailer court—and he probably won't sign off on her claim anyway. She's seen him before—three years ago according to her chart. He cut her off then. Stan never signs off on these claims. That's why we send them his way. She wants to see Francis Zeller. Francis is an older and more sympathetic psychiatrist. Stan and I like to do imitations of her sometimes over a beer down at Woody's. We send fewer and fewer clients to Francis since she became a pushover after her own bout with depression.

It's hard *not* to get depressed over this job. I wrap up my interview with the woman and her child of indeterminate sex and send them packing with a hearty handshake —back out into the freezing rain—Mr. Friendly.

Amanda Spaulding is dead.

Terry didn't tell me this right away. His email started out with a joke. It's the funniest joke in the world, actually. I had already heard it. It was the result of an Oxford

Mr. Friendly

or Cambridge study on what's funny—what makes us laugh. And this one was the funniest joke in the world or maybe the second funniest. I can't remember.

I don't think I laughed as hard as I did when Amanda Spaulding fell down the church steps in her bridesmaid's gown during Jim's wedding. But that was different.

After the joke, he didn't just write, *Amanda Spaulding is dead*. He said, "I've got some bad news. Our old friend, Amanda Spaulding passed away."

Passed away.

It's not like him to say *passed away*. Of course, I don't really know him any more. I still think of the way he was in high school. He was my friend, but a guy you could never turn your back on. If you did, he'd do something to you—slap you in the back of the head, or give you a wedgie, or knock your books out of your hands.

I remember the time we were shooting baskets, practicing our moves for team tryouts the next day. I broke his big toe he wouldn't give my ball back when I had to get home. I said, "I'm outta here," and foolishly turned to leave. When he jumped on my back, I got pissed off and threw him over my shoulders. He landed in front of me, rolling around, screaming in pain. It took him years to get over missing basketball tryouts.

Back then he would have said, Amanda bought the farm, or Amanda croaked.

I shuffle a few papers before heading home. Stephanie wiggles over to my cubicle. I sneak glances at her all day long since she came on board in November. She's aware of my interest. Sometimes I think about the unfairness of relationships between men and women. I notice Stephanie because she's young and pretty. I don't give Doris or Sandy a second look. Doris is my age. Sandy's younger than Doris but kind of dumpy. In a few more years she'll look like our clients.

I should go home and run. Sitting on my ass all day, I'm going to look like them soon.

"What's up?" Stephanie says. "Wanna go get a beer?"

"Can't. Ellen's got people coming over tonight. I gotta help clean the house."

She pouts at me. "Boo hoo," she says.

"Rain check?" I say.

"Sure. Hey, I watched a movie last night, *American Beauty*. It sort of reminded me of you. Have you seen it?"

As she is saying this, Sandy walks past on her way out.

"Night," she says, with a look of disgust that I'm sure is intended for Stephanie, maybe me too.

"Night, Sandy," we say at the same time, all smiles.

"No," I say. "Haven't seen it." (I've seen it.)

"You really should. I'd like to know what you think." She smiles. "I'll bring it so you can watch it before I have to take it back."

In the movie, the pathetic numb male lead falls ridiculously for his daughter's teenaged friend. What Stephanie is saying is that:

I'm pathetic.

She wants to fuck me anyway.

"Sure," I say, "Bring it tomorrow and I'll get it back to you by the weekend."

"Night."

"Night."

When I get home, there's a note.

I've gone to the grocery. You need to vacuum the living room and mop the kitchen floor. Do a good job this time. You don't have time to run. It's icy out there anyway.

I put on my running gear, go out the door and slip on the ice. I feel the pain in the spot in my back where I had my surgery years ago. Shit. I don't need this again.

Mr. Friendly

It's that same spot again. Nevertheless, my theory is to run it out. I'll make the pain submit to my will. At last it seems to subside and I find myself thinking about Amanda again.

She's dead.

Dead is something we don't accept easily. The last time I saw her was at the only class reunion I ever went to. The twentieth, I think. Some people looked the same. Apparently I looked better, because everybody said, *you've lost weight*. I must have been fat in high school. I don't remember that. Bill Delaney looked like he could have been my dad. But Amanda—wow. She must've been wanting to show off. For a dentist, she was hot. There were no other women there with bare midriffs.

I turn up Rosemont Circle. The pain has eased now and my stride returns to normal.

Flirting with her at the reunion, twenty years too late was so easy, but there was no time—one night at a class reunion. Why had I been so shy in high school when I blew the opportunities she gave me? Like that time in the AV equipment room. My nerdy AV equipment manager job didn't really require an assistant, but when Mrs. Hopkins assigned Amanda to help me, I wasn't about to object.

"I want to show you something," she said as I struggled to instruct her, with shaking fingers, how to thread the 16 mm projector in the dark.

She unbuttoned her blouse and pulled it open.

"Don't you think this is pretty?"

"I . . .I ...yes."

She meant the pink lacy bra that glowed with each flicker of light from the noisy projector. There could have been more I guess, but I was petrified. I looked away and when I looked back everything was back in place as though it had never happened. It was never mentioned again until twenty years later—me the actuary working on his second marriage—she the San Francisco dentist working on her second divorce.

"Do you remember when I was your AV assistant?" she asked me over a rum and coke and the 70's musical nostalgia blaring from the PA system.

"Every second of it,' I lied.

"I really had a crush on you. But you never seemed interested."

"I'm interested now."

"What are we going to do about this?" she asked.

I try to remember as I hit the two-mile turning point of my run, did we ever even kiss?

Here's what we did. We got drunk. Even that night when I'm sure we both wanted each other badly, I can't remember kissing her. She wanted me to come to San Francisco but I never did.

That twice-postponed love affair is really over now. Death is the final blow to romance. What did she die of? Cancer? Accident? Murder?

At the twenty-year reunion they read the death list. Out of all those people, only four had kicked the bucket. There was the fat gay guy who committed suicide. Judy Bellows—cancer and Steve Leslie. Steve froze to death on his own doorstep. I found out later that he was an alcoholic and that lots of alcoholics freeze to death—a hundred or a thousand a year—some big stupid number. Then there was Benny Meadows, of course. We could have predicted how he would go. Benny always played with guns. Shot himself in the foot when he was in grade school, accidental discharge of a shotgun into his leg during high school. Then when he was about thirty, he finished the job once and for all.

I remember the night my big class graduated, making a point to scan my gowned classmates to see if I knew each one of them. I counted four that I had no memory of ever seeing before. I don't think I saw Amanda at all that

Mr. Friendly

night.

Oh shit! The pain is back. I have to stop running. I'd really like to lie down but I don't. I only have a mile to go before I get home. Every step is excruciating. It's making me sweat profusely. When I get to the house I stop. My leg has gone numb. I try to move my foot. I start walking up the street and notice that with each step, my left foot wiggles then comes down with a sharp flat slap. I picture my own MRI scan. The nerve is pinned against my vertebrae by my newly herniated disk. Which one, I wonder? L-5? S-1? When my foot hits the ground it is turned at a fifteen-degree angle to the left. I test it by starting to run again. Slap. Slap.

I left the house miserable and returned horrible.

What will Stephanie think of me now? I wonder if she'll mind my useless left leg. I imagine her snuggled against my chest at the Hampton Inn. She feels sorry for me, a pathetic cripple.

"Wanna hear the funniest joke in the world?" I'll say.

"Sure," she'll say, all sleepy and warm.

"These two guys go out duck hunting. One of them suddenly grabs at his chest and falls over. The other one remembers his cell phone and calls 911—I'm out in the woods hunting with my friend, he says. I think he's had a heart attack. I think he's dead—Now stay clam sir, the operator says. First of all, let's make sure he's really dead—OK, the guy says, and the phone goes quiet. Then there's this gun shot. He comes back on the phone—OK, the guy says. Now what?"

Maybe that's what happened to Benny Meadows.